CHRISTMAS ON THE CAPE

A NOVELLA

PERIWINKLE SHORES
BOOK ONE

ANNIE CABOT

CABOT PUBLISHING GROUP

CHAPTER 1

*R*achel Adams stood in front of her aunt's cottage and shook her head. Holding her baby Everly in her arms, she walked toward the back of the building and wondered if she'd made a mistake. Her sisters Lucy and Hannah pretended nothing was wrong.

"I don't know, you guys. The last time I visited Aunt Kathleen, this house looked a lot better than it does now. It's going to take every penny I have and then some to fix it."

Hannah tried to make light of the situation.

"Oh, it's not that bad, just a few cosmetic touches and it will be good as new."

Rachel looked at Hannah in disbelief and then turned to Lucy. She depended on Lucy to be the reasonable one, but even she remained infuriatingly optimistic.

"Ok, maybe it needs a bit more than changing wallpaper and rugs, but I think it's perfect for you and Everly. We'll help in any way we can. I know lots of people in town who wouldn't charge you too much for some of the repairs."

Rachel handed Everly to Lucy and walked across the street. Looking up, she pointed to the roof.

"How old do you think that is? A new roof is going to cost me at least eight thousand dollars."

Lucy tickled Everly's cheek and Rachel watched as the two burst into loud giggles. Everly had been such a blessing. Her heart swelled knowing her child would be surrounded by so much love now that she was back on the Cape.

Hannah joined Lucy and Everly in playful tickles. The baby was bundled up to cover every inch of her skin. Her face was the only exposed part of her body, and by now, her cheeks had turned a deep shiny pink.

Rachel took off her leather gloves and sighed. Walking to the front door, she pushed the hood of her winter coat down.

"We might as well go inside and see what else needs work."

Her sisters followed her into the house, with Everly laughing at Hannah who was making funny faces at her.

Rachel was pleasantly surprised that the heat had been turned on. Images of water damage from burst pipes had dominated her thoughts when the temperature plummeted the day before. She realized Lucy had thought the same thing and said so.

"I assume I have you to thank for the heat?"

Lucy nodded. "I ran over here as soon as I heard the weather forecast. I didn't really do anything. The heat was already on, I just checked on it and ran the water in all the sinks and bathtub for a bit."

Her aunt Kathleen wasn't the neatest person, with stacks of magazine and papers everywhere. The clutter was overwhelming.

"Am I crazy or would you say that Aunt Kathleen was a hoarder? Look at these magazines. Some of them are from the nineteen-sixties."

Hannah examined the figurines inside a glass cabinet.

"Looks like she collected lots of things. I know this woman who lives a few houses from me who does the same thing. She goes to all the yard sales, but I don't think she sells anything. She just brings it all home and watches it pile up. I can't imagine what her place looks like."

The women continued their inspection of the house including Everly, whose head turned left and right to take in her new surroundings. The inside had fared much better than the outside. Rachel could see herself living here but would need to remove all the furniture and start fresh.

"Check around for any water damage. That's my biggest concern."

Everly started to fuss, so Lucy gave the baby to Rachel.

"She wants her mama."

Rachel took off Everly's coat and then her own. Holding the baby close she found a soft, cushioned rocking chair. The two of them snuggled as Rachel thought back to her visits to the house over the years. She could see her aunt in this very chair, rocking her sister Hannah as Rachel entertained Lucy on the rug. It had been only two weeks since their aunt died, but she could still hear Kathleen's voice.

"You can take the girl out of Cape Cod, but you can't take Cape Cod out of the girl."

Rachel's family had lived on the Cape since before she was born. Her memories were filled with happy times and lots of lobster bakes and dancing under the string lights in the backyard.

When Rachel married and moved away from Periwinkle Shores she was twenty-two. Later, her sister Lucy went off to college and then came back home to be close to family and never left.

Their parents divorced when Hannah was still in high school. It was the four of them for several years but then their mother passed away of a sudden stroke five years ago. Their father remarried and moved to California with his new wife, leaving his grown daughters to figure life out on their own.

There was ten years between Rachel and Lucy and seven between Lucy and Hannah. They thought it strange that their parents had them so many years apart, but there was much about their parents' marriage that confused them.

After Rachel married, she moved north to Andover, Massachusetts where her husband's family had lived for decades. Although boyfriends came and went, Lucy and Hannah seemed content to remain single, living carefree lives on the Cape. They checked on their mother's sister and brother often and would keep Rachel up to date on their heath. Kathleen and her brother Matthew had never married and lived together their whole lives.

Matthew died of a heart attack several years ago, and now, Kathleen was gone from the same ailment. What pained Rachel the most was that she didn't get to say goodbye to her aunt.

Hannah and Lucy spent time with Kathleen since they lived so close, but a massive heart attack took their aunt away in an instant and there was little they could do to save her.

When it happened, Rachel was still dealing with her divorce and a new baby, making it impossible to rush down to the Cape to be with her sisters. Instead, she talked to them on the phone and made her way south for the funeral.

Everyone on their mother's side of the family died before they were sixty years old, a fact that worried Rachel, not for her health alone, but for Everly's. There wasn't much Rachel wanted from Everly's father, but if his genetics helped her child live a long life, she'd gladly accept it.

Rachel was shocked to learn that Kathleen had left the house to her. Although they loved each other, Rachel was hardly close to her aunt and rarely visited. If anyone deserved the inheritance, it was Lucy, who worshipped Kathleen.

Both Lucy and Hannah had their own homes and were happy for Rachel when the details of Kathleen's generosity were revealed. However, why Kathleen thought the house should be hers, she had no idea.

Maybe she took pity on Everly and me and thought we needed to come home to Periwinkle Shores.

The stress and trauma of the last year had taken a toll on Rachel. Her husband had never wanted children and had surgery to prevent an accidental pregnancy. He'd done it without Rachel's knowledge which drove a wedge between them.

Trust had become a major issue in their marriage, and regardless of his procedure, Rachel had become pregnant. Brian insisted that she'd had an affair and that the child was not his. He couldn't accept that the surgery had been a failure, and even went so far as to insist Rachel take a paternity test.

Rachel saw the pregnancy as a gift from God and couldn't have been more excited about the situation. She'd naively believed that the baby would bring them closer and counted on her husband falling in love with the infant as soon as he held the baby in his arms.

Nothing could have been further from reality. Instead, Brian left her and Everly and said that he wanted nothing to do with the child. When the paternity test proved that her was indeed the father, Brian finally agreed to pay child support.

Looking back over the events of the last year, Rachel had finally come to terms with her situation. She loved every bit of her pregnancy and despite her soon-to-be ex-husband's attitude toward her, she found peace and stability with her baby.

She'd filed to change her legal name back to her maiden one in part because she didn't want anything to do with Brian. The more important reason was that she didn't want Everly to have his last name. The thought of Everly having Ellis as a last name depressed Rachel. Everly Ellis wouldn't do and since Brian was fine with the change, she signed the birth certificate for her child as Everly Brooke Adams.

How often she'd look at Everly and say, "It's you and me, kid", or "We're going to be just fine."

Everly would look up at her with her big blue eyes and smile.

Rachel convinced herself that the two of them would take on the world and were part of an exclusive club that no one was allowed to enter. Their bond was strong, and she couldn't imagine her life without the nineteen-pound bundle of joy in her arms.

Hannah and Lucy came into the room and dropped onto the sofa.

Lucy frowned and looked at Rachel.

"Do you want the good news or the bad news first?"

"Give me the bad news first."

"There are two water stains on the ceiling above the second-floor bathroom. They're not old stains either. I touched them and they're wet. If I had to guess, I'd say the water is coming through the roof. So, you were right, you'll probably have to fork over a bunch of money to replace it. You're going to need to get a plumber in here as soon as possible to check on it though because there's always a chance that it might be something else."

"Is that it or is there more bad news?"

Hannah answered first. "I smell something awful in the laundry room. I can't even describe it, but it's pretty bad. Probably something else for the plumber to look at, either that or an animal died in there."

Rachel wanted to scream but Everly had fallen asleep in her arms, so she did her best to remain calm.

"What's the good news?"

Lucy sat up and smiled.

"There are two bottles of wine in the kitchen and a couple of coupons for free pizza."

Lucy Adams pulled her long brown hair up into a messy bun and pushed her dark-rimmed glasses up on her nose. She'd spent the morning going over her manuscript one last time before sending it to her editor. More than once this morning her cell phone interrupted her work which frustrated her.

She loved getting her first draft out before its due date, but this project was late, and it was her own fault. Her sister Rachel had moved back to Periwinkle Shores and although she was excited to have her sister return home, she knew there was much to do to get Rachel settled in.

She pressed the send icon and sat back in her chair. It was her practice to pour a glass of wine the minute she sent the manuscript to her editor, but it was too early in the day, so she decided to put that on hold and poured herself a cup of coffee instead.

Over the years Lucy and her sister Hannah would drive up to see Rachel. It was rare for Rachel to drive to them and Lucy blamed Rachel's ex-husband for that. To get to Rachel's home in Andover took about two and a half hours from Periwinkle Shores, and that's only if the traffic was light. She knew her sister missed the Cape and it infuriated her that Brian's controlling ways prevented Rachel from visiting. He never let Rachel out of his sight, but there was little Lucy could do about it.

Brian had been a terrible husband and human being in Lucy's eyes. He constantly put Rachel down, telling her that she was incapable of succeeding at anything. He criticized her at every turn. His behavior infuriated Lucy and more than once she thought seriously of driving up to Andover and rescuing her sister from her prison. It took a pregnancy to release Rachel from Brian's grip. In Lucy's eyes, her niece Everly saved Rachel from a terrible future.

Lucy got up from her chair and carried her coffee outside to her small patio. Her Cape-styled home was small by most people's standards, but it suited her perfectly. She loved living alone. The quiet privacy of her property afforded her countless hours of solitude in which to write.

As a self-published romance fiction author, Lucy Adams had a successful career. She'd struggled for years trying to get an agent after querying publishing houses and finally gave up when she heard about self-publishing from her friend, a successful author in her own right, from Newport, Rhode Island.

After publishing four books under her own name, Lucy was hooked. She loved communicating with her readers and felt that each one was a member of her extended family. Her sister Hannah had the task of reading the first draft of Lucy's books, and had become a valuable assistant in Lucy's small, but flourishing publishing world.

Hannah had been eager to help Lucy, and would read the stories, a few chapters at a time at the end of the day working at her spa, *The Pink Seashell.* The spa had a steady group of repeat customers and in Lucy's opinion, it was a great place for the local women to socialize and gossip while getting their hair, nails and facials done. Hannah kept Lucy up to date on all the latest Periwinkle Shores news, and they spent hours laughing over some of the outrageous and embellished stories.

Now that Rachel was back home, the three sisters could resume their traditions and share childhood memories that they'd pass down to Everly. Lucy couldn't wait for summer when the three of them could take her down to the beach and introduce her to the Cape Cod National Seashore. Collecting seashells and building sandcastles were family traditions growing up, and soon they would become part of Everly's world too.

Known in Periwinkle Shores as the Sea Glass Girls because of their huge collection over the years, Lucy, Rachel and Hannah added a forth to their exclusive club. Little Everly was now one of the Sea Glass Girls. Rachel may have navigated off-course for a while, but she was back, and the Adams women were stronger for it.

Brian would never again bother Rachel, and if he dared show his face in Periwinkle Shores, he'd have to go through Lucy and Hannah to get to her. Lucy smiled thinking how she'd love nothing better than to see him try. She hadn't had a good fight in a long, long time.

CHAPTER 2

*H*annah Adams smiled at Mr. Wilkins as he passed *The Pink Seashell.* The red Christmas buttons on his hat blinked on and off and even though it was a blustery, cold day, he didn't slow down one bit.

She could always tell the time of day as soon as she saw him cross the street heading toward the spa. He walked with purpose, as if he had some place important to go, but to hear people tell it, Josiah Wilkins walked just to get the exercise. He lived alone and the only time he saw anyone except his cat was on his morning walk.

Hannah scrubbed the last streak on the window and got up from the floor and carried her bucket of cleaning supplies to the counter. Now that the window was clean, she opened the first box filled with Christmas decorations.

Her employee and friend, Jill, shook her head.

"I feel bad for him. How old do you think he is?"

Hannah shrugged, "No idea. If I had to guess, I'd say maybe in his late seventies. I wouldn't feel too bad for him. He's always smiling and seems happy. I assume the red hat is his way of getting in the Christmas spirit."

"Speaking of Christmas, I haven't even started shopping yet. How about you?"

Hannah shook her head. "Nope. Now that Rachel's back, Lucy and I have been focused on helping her settle in. I'm excited to buy Christmas gifts for Everly, though. It's going to be a blast watching her open them."

Jill finished stocking the shelves with calendula body lotion.

"So, how's your sister making out? Do you think she'll sell your aunt's house and get another property?"

"I doubt it. She wants to fix it up and live there. I'm glad too. I didn't want to see that house go to a stranger. It feels right having one of us living there."

"You've lived alone for a long time, Hannah. How is it having Rachel and the baby stay with you?"

"Honestly, I don't mind. Everly is great and Rachel helps out by cooking. I don't remember the last time I ate such delicious home-cooked meals. She should open a restaurant with her talent."

Jill nodded. "I think it's a great idea. Not that Periwinkle Shores needs another restaurant, but Rachel will need to get a job at some point. She might as well start her own business. I'm going to mention it to her the next time I see her."

Hannah considered what Jill had said. Neither Lucy nor Hannah put any pressure on Rachel to find a job, but Hannah knew her sister. Rachel loved being a teacher, but in moving to the Cape with a new baby she had to put her career on hold.

Once her sister settled in, it was anyone's guess what Rachel would do for work. For now, Rachel would stay with Hannah until repairs on Kathleen's house were completed.

The bells above the spa's front door rang and Lily Jacobson and four of her friends giggled as they entered the spa. Lily was the mayor's daughter and was here for her bachelorette party pampering.

Hannah walked behind the counter.

"Hello, ladies. I'll check you in. You can go on back and put on your robes and slippers. Jill and Sierra will take care of you."

Jill leaned close to Hannah and whispered, "Do you think we should pipe in Christmas music instead of the usual?"

Hannah shook her head. "No way. People come into the spa to get away from Christmas for a few minutes. Not these ladies, but most. I can't envision Jingle Bells relaxing anyone."

After she finished with the appointment book, Hannah went into her office and closed the door. She had bookkeeping to do and needed a few minutes alone to think.

She'd never said a word to either Lucy or Rachel, but the last three months of her business were a struggle. More money went out than came in, and although she could float for a few months, the spa soon wouldn't survive the decline in sales. No matter how many times she went over the numbers, the end result was always the same.

Being the youngest of the three girls, Hannah worked hard to keep up with her sisters. Petite with shoulder length blond hair, she'd take two steps for every one of her sister's. They used it to their advantage when they were children.

With so many years between their birth dates, it was easy to avoid becoming much of a nuisance. Never wanting their little sister to hang with them, Lucy and Rachel would walk so fast to get away from her that Hannah would give up as soon as they rounded a corner and were out of sight.

Being shorter wasn't the only thing that kept her from joining in. Slightly overweight since childhood, Hannah never caught the ball or ran the bases like her sisters. Instead, she opted for more sedentary activities which almost always included eating extra of everything.

Along with the weight gain came the inevitable bullying at school. Her only saving grace was that both Rachel and Lucy each had a strong right hook and would use it if necessary. No one dared bother Hannah after one unfortunate incident when too much teasing convinced Lucy to act. Showing up at Hannah's school, Lucy stuck her foot out and watched as Victoria Allen face-planted in front of the other kids. As Lucy put it, it was one of the best memories of her childhood, and Hannah was forever grateful.

However, just because no one upset Hannah with nasty insults, hardly anyone included her in any school activity or club. All that changed the moment Hannah noticed Ethan Manning. The fact that he'd dominated her thinking around the clock kept her focused on things other than food. As soon as her weight dropped, she became motivated to get in shape.

With the fast metabolism of youth, and a desire to learn everything about cosmetics, Hannah changed everything about herself on the outside. The inside however, was another matter. Painfully shy, she didn't know what to do with her newfound beauty. As soon as boys started noticing her, she panicked and refused to make eye contact with them.

When Ethan asked her to the school prom, she'd nearly died from the shock. Somewhere, deep inside, she found the courage to accept, and spent the days leading up to the event begging her mother to buy her the most beautiful dress she could find. As soon as they found the perfect dress, Lucy taught her how to apply makeup. The prom had been a wonderful success and after her first goodnight kiss, Hannah believed she might have a social life after all.

As it turned out, her social life was an unexpected problem. Parties and missing classes proved her downfall and in her senior year there'd been a real chance that she wouldn't graduate with her peers. Her parents were in the middle of a divorce and so, she didn't get the structure and attention she desperately needed. Adding a few summer classes, Hannah did graduate, but not with her friends, a mistake she regretted deeply.

Except for a part-time job at the local supermarket, she'd had zero skills and even less ambition until she saw an ad in the paper for a manicurist. She didn't have any experience except a passion for cosmetics and other beauty products, but it was enough to land her the job. The owner was desperate to fill the vacancy and Hannah happened to be at the right place at the right time.

In no time at all, she found her calling. Going back to school to be a hairdresser, followed by getting a certificate as a licensed cosmetologist, Hannah excelled. No one was prouder of her than her sisters, and with a little financial help from her aunt Kathleen, opened *The Pink Seashell*.

Now, she struggled to keep the spa afloat, and was terrified to admit to her sisters that she'd failed, once again. A knock on her door interrupted her thoughts.

"Come on in."

Rachel poked her head inside.

"Hey, Hannah. Got a minute?"

Hannah got up from her desk.

"Hey, of course."

Lucy followed behind Rachel carrying Everly.

"Wow, both of you visiting me in the middle of the day. Must be something important if both of my sisters land in my office before noon. What's up?"

She could tell that neither of her sisters wanted to be the first to speak.

"Come on, you guys. What's going on?"

Lucy smiled and leaned against the wall letting Rachel and Everly take the chair.

"Well, Rachel and I have found someone to repair the roof. Because it's so cold and we've probably got snow coming, they can't completely redo the whole thing right now. Instead, we're just going to patch the immediate problem so Rachel can get through the winter."

Rachel interrupted. "He said there's all kinds of issues because of the cold, so for now, we're just going to do the small repair."

Uneasy, Hannah was afraid to ask her next question.

"He who?"

No one said anything for a minute, but then Hannah could see Lucy looking at Rachel for help.

"That's why we stopped by," Lucy said.

Rachel answered her. "Oliver Mason."

Hannah started to pace the floor.

"No, no, no. Not him. Anyone but him."

Lucy reached for Hannah, "You're being unreasonable. He's the best contractor within fifty miles and you know it."

Rachel tried to help.

"It's my fault, Hannah. I contacted him without knowing that you two had dated in the past. Lucy told me about your relationship with him, and I told her that if it was a real problem, we can hire someone else."

Rachel looked at Lucy. "I told you this was a mistake."

Lucy wasn't giving up.

"No, it's not. Listen to me, Hannah. You'll never have to see Oliver at all. It's not like he's doing work on your place. Not only that, but he's also willing to charge Rachel only for materials and nothing for labor. Why make her pay so much more when she doesn't have to, just because you're being stubborn."

Hannah's eyes grew wide. "Stubborn? You think I'm being stubborn?"

Lucy rolled her eyes, looked at Rachel, and shrugged.

"I give up."

"Fine. I'll look for someone else. Come on, Lucy. Let's go."

Rachel started for the door, but Hannah stopped her.

"Wait... I'm sorry, Rachel. I didn't mean to mess things up for you. Go ahead and hire him. Just understand that I won't be able to come to your house when he's there. Also, please don't share anything about my life with him. I'm pretty sure he's going to ask you if I'm seeing someone, which I'm not, but he doesn't need to know that."

Lucy smiled and patted Hannah on the back, and Rachel nodded in agreement.

"Absolutely. I promise never to bring your name up, and if he does, I'll just explain that I'm not at liberty to speak about others without their approval."

Hannah threw her arms up in the air.

"No. Don't say that."

Rachel shook her head. "No? I don't say that?"

"No. That sounds like we've talked and I told you not to say anything to him."

Hannah was beside herself, and neither of her sisters seemed to understand her despair.

"Wait. I've got it. Just say, you don't know anything. That's better."

Lucy and Rachel looked confused but didn't dare continue to probe her for more. She'd given her permission to hire Oliver Mason and that should be more than enough to satisfy everyone, at least for now.

CHAPTER 3

*T*wo dead rats were responsible for the awful smell coming from the laundry room. Oliver Mason disposed of them and looked at Rachel and tried not to laugh.

"At least now you won't have to wonder where the smell is coming from."

Rachel held her stomach and tried not to vomit.

'That's disgusting. How did they get in there?"

"The question isn't how they got in, but why they couldn't get back out. Looks like your aunt hired someone to put a wire mesh in the opening. The way it works is that the rodent doesn't feel any resistance leaving the house but if they tried to get back in, they'd be going against the grain making it painful for them. Whoever installed it put it in backwards. The rats encountered resistance trying to get out."

"You mean they were already in the house before it was installed?"

Oliver nodded. "That's right. Not only that but your aunt left poison in the laundry room, and the rats found it."

Rachel wondered what other surprises were left for her to find.

"I'm sorry you had to deal with that but thank you. I'm not sure what I would have done if I found them myself," Rachel said.

"No problem. It's not the first time I've found something like this. Comes with the territory. Anyway, I'm done for today. I'll try to be back tomorrow. Also, I've given your name to a friend of mine. He's the best plumber in town. I asked him to stop by tomorrow to take a look at a couple of spots that aren't connected to the roof. You might have another leak. If I had to guess, it's probably coming from the washing machine. His name is Jack Harris. He should be by sometime in the morning if that works for you."

"Yes, that's fine. Thank you. This house is old, and my aunt probably didn't do much work around here after Uncle Matthew died. I want to get this place up and running as soon as possible. I can't stay at my sister's house forever. Everly and I need our own home."

"Not to worry. It won't be long before you and your little girl are happily settled in."

Oliver had a pleasant way about him. His light brown hair was a bit longer than she was used to seeing in men, but the wavy layered look softened his rugged face. His fair completion and blue eyes probably had most of the women in Periwinkle Shores falling in love with him. He was definitely handsome, and she could see why her sister Hannah was attracted to him.

So far, Hannah refused to share her feelings about Oliver with either Lucy or her, but there was no way Rachel would wait any longer to get to the bottom of Hannah's avoiding him. She didn't have to come up with an excuse to talk about his dating Hannah. Oliver seemed anxious to talk about her.

"So, I haven't seen Lucy or Hannah in a while. How are they doing?" Oliver asked.

She thought it funny that Oliver included Lucy in his probing. The disguise didn't fool her.

"Oh, they're doing well. I'm so glad that I'm finally home. I've missed my family. Christmas is going to be so much more fun for both Everly and me this year. Having Lucy and Hannah nearby is such a blessing."

Oliver nodded. "I'm sure your sisters are happy to have you home as well. What's Hannah been up to lately? I didn't know if you knew this or not, but she and I used to date a while back."

Rachel went along with her promise to Hannah not to appear that she had any information about the man. A small white lie wouldn't hurt anything.

"No, I didn't know that. How long ago was that?"

"We split up about a month ago."

"A month ago?"

Rachel was under the impression that it had been much longer than that.

Oliver leaned against the kitchen wall.

"She broke up with me through a text."

"What? That doesn't sound like Hannah. Why would she do such a thing?"

Oliver shrugged.

"You're asking the wrong person. I have no idea. One minute we were really close and the next, she doesn't want to see me anymore. I wish I knew what I'd done wrong, but I haven't a clue."

She could tell that his statement left room for her to intervene.

"Would you like me to find out?"

Oliver's face lit up.

"Would you?"

The poor guy was obviously in love with Hannah, and Rachel hated the idea that such a love would end just because her sister refused to give him another chance.

"Of course. I'll see what I can do."

Oliver looked and acted like he was twelve years old, and she marveled at the coincidence that on more than one occasion, her sister Hannah looked and acted the exact same way.

They were perfect for each other.

Lucy sat inside the playpen with her niece and put two round plastic donuts on her head.

"Go ahead, Everly. Try to knock them down."

Everly stuck her hand out above Lucy's head and knocked the donuts off, giggling every time they fell. The two of them had been playing like this for the last fifteen minutes, and Rachel smiled, pleased that her sister had yet to lose patience with the game.

"Thank you so much for watching her this morning. I'm thrilled that I've now got a plumber, but not so happy about the fact that I need one."

"No problem. Everly and I are having a blast. I don't think I've ever played inside a playpen before. At least not since I was an infant myself. You'll like Jack Harris. His family owns Stellar Seas Vineyards, or what used to be a vineyard. You must have seen it out on Rte. 6 near Truro."

"If his family owns a vineyard, why is he about to become my new plumber?"

Lucy laughed.

"Well, the vineyard hasn't been in operation for years, and the truth is there isn't much Jack doesn't do around Periwinkle Shores. I hate to use the expression, 'Jack of all trades', but it's really true in his case. You'll see what I mean once you meet him."

Rachel grabbed her keys and gave Everly a kiss on the head.

"I shouldn't be too long. Thanks again for watching her for me."

Rachel stepped outside and her face was immediately hit with large snowflakes. She stuck out her tongue, something she'd done since she was a child, and walked to her car. She drove through the center of town on her way to her new house.

Every store was decorated with Christmas lights, bells and balsam fir, and she smiled when she saw *The Pink Seashell's* colorful lights around the front door. Hannah loved Christmas, and Rachel figured that her sister must have started decorating the day before, not after, Thanksgiving.

A banner advertising the town's Christmas Stroll waved back and forth in the wind. The Stroll was a Periwinkle Shores tradition, and Rachel smiled thinking about past years when she helped prepare for the big day.

She pulled into her driveway and parked next to a white truck. A picture of pipes and a sink along with the words, Jack Harris - Plumber, were advertised on the driver's side door.

A man with dark brown hair under a baseball cap and a scruffy beard sat inside. He waved at her, and she stood at the front door waiting for him to get out of his truck.

"I'm so sorry, I had to get my sister to watch my daughter. Have you been waiting long?"

He smiled and shook his head.

"Nope. I just got here."

They walked inside the house and Rachel rubbed her arms.

"I know you want to get started right away, but would you care for a cup of tea or coffee to warm up? I can't get over how cold it's been the last two weeks."

"No, Thank you. I'm fine. It's nice to see you again."

"I'm sorry? Have we met?"

He looked down at his boots and shook his head.

"We were in the same graduating class in high school. I'm not surprised you don't remember me. You were very popular in school, and I was pretty shy."

Rachel felt awful for not recognizing Jack, but the truth was that she hung around with a handful of friends who didn't often accept outsiders. If Jack was shy, it was a good bet that he didn't meet the click's standards.

"I'm so sorry. I've no doubt I was obnoxious back then. You know what it's like being in a group where everyone tries to impress each other. It's a lot like a cult."

Jack shook his head.

"No, I don't."

This isn't going well. I expect my plumbing bill will be twice as much as his usual bill for such work.

"The truth was that I thought you were out of my league being a cheerleader and all. If I thought you'd have given me the time of day, I would have approached you the first time I saw you. I actually sent you an invitation to a party at my house, because my father told me to."

"What?"

Jack nodded.

"It's true. It was my birthday party and we were in the fifth grade. My father insisted that I send you an invitation. I did, but you never responded."

"Oh, no. That's awful. I can't believe I'd ever turn down an invitation for cake and ice cream."

"That's what I thought too, but you didn't even turn it down, you just ignored it."

""How in the world did your father even know who I was?"

"No clue. I'm not really surprised though. Martin Harris knows everyone in town. I bet he was a friend of your parents. If I knew how pretty you'd turn out to be in high school, I might have delivered the invitation in person."

Rachel couldn't ignore how handsome Jack was, but she also didn't miss the fact that he was flirting with her, and she didn't like it one bit. Instead, she decided to play nice and apologize for being insulting as a child.

"Well, we were stupid kids. When I think back to those years,

I cringe. I hope I wasn't too unbearable. Will you forgive me if I was?"

"I'm pretty sure it's forgotten, but just in case it isn't, I'm still going to charge you for my services."

They laughed at his joke, although Rachel was certain he was only half-kidding.

"Well, I better get to work. I've been in this house before, so I know my way around."

"Oh, you have?"

"Yes, I came by to help your aunt and uncle on occasion. They did a lot for the community and I was glad to help them when they needed it."

"I didn't know that. I'll leave you to your work, then."

She watched Jack move around the house as if he lived there. From one bathroom to the other and then out to his truck, she could tell that he knew what he was doing. Wrapping her arms around her body, she smiled, thinking that her wish to be in the house long before Christmas might actually happen.

When he was done, Jack called out to her.

"You have one small leak in one of the pipes leading from the washing machine. It's no bigger than the head of a pin, but over time it's made the floor wet and weak. I repaired the pipe, but you'll need someone to fix the floor. I can give Oliver a call and see if he can come over and have a look."

"Would you? That would be great. The sooner the better."

"I'll call him right now. Hang on."

Jack went outside to call Oliver. Other than this latest repair, she felt certain that she and Everly could move in any time. Her excitement building, Rachel began thinking of furniture and decorating ideas. She'd hired movers to take out what she didn't want and expected them the next morning. Although the inside would have little furniture this holiday, having a Christmas tree was top on her to-do list.

"Oliver was planning on being here tomorrow anyway. He'll be here at two o'clock if that works for you."

"That's perfect. I'll be here all day tomorrow since I've got movers coming. Tell him that I'll see him then."

Jack finished his call with Oliver and then collected his tools and carried them to his truck. Pulling her sweater close, Rachel walked toward him.

"What do I owe you? Will you take a check?"

He smiled and got inside the truck. Looking at her through the open window, he said, "I was only kidding about charging you. Consider it a welcome home gift. I'm glad you're back in Periwinkle Shores, Rachel. Don't be a stranger, ok?"

She nodded and smiled at him. "I won't. Thank you, Jack."

She watched as he drove down the street. She was angry at herself for finding Jack so attractive. It wasn't his charm that unnerved her, but rather her inclination to even consider him as someone for whom she could have romantic feelings. Ridiculous as it seemed, Rachel admonished herself for glancing at his hand in search of a wedding ring.

After everything she'd been through with her ex-husband, she vowed to stay clear of the opposite sex. She didn't need a man in her and Everly's life. Every awful thing her ex had said to her over the years came flooding back. His opinion of her dominated her thinking for so long, she'd struggled to believe she was capable of anything

Now, she and her daughter would find their way together, and with her sisters' help would manage anything life threw their way. They were the Sea Glass Girls after all, and the spirit of their aunt Kathleen, the original Sea Glass Girl, would guide the way.

More than anything, she wanted to set a good example for her daughter. Rachel would do everything she could to strengthen Everly's confidence. She'd tell her daughter that as long as she worked hard and never gave up, she could accomplish anything she set her mind and heart on.

This was Rachel's singular focus, and for all his charm, Jack Harris would never convince her to think of him as anything but her plumber.

She had more important things to think about including making plans for her future. Wondering about someone who so obviously thought he could get any woman he wanted was a waste of time.

That self-deprecating 'oh gosh you were out of my league in high school' act didn't fool her one bit. Rachel would stay clear of Jack Harris and his good looks. Unfortunately for her, she lived in a very small town.

CHAPTER 4

$\mathcal{R}$achel took comfort in the fact that living on the water meant the air was warmer than it was where she lived before. Waiting for the movers, she sat at the bay window drinking her coffee. Trying to stay warm, her fingers wrapped around the cup. She thought about her aunt Kathleen and imagined her sitting in this very spot.

Her cell phone rang just as the movers arrived.

"Hey, Hannah. What's up?"

"Can I come by and take a quick look at Aunt Kathleen's stuff before the movers get there? I know I should have done this already, but first I wanted to make sure that you-know-who wasn't around."

"You better get over here right now because the truck just pulled up."

"I'm coming. Don't throw anything away. I can be there in three minutes."

"Ok, I'll have them start with the old junk in the basement. You don't want any of that stuff, right?"

"Right. That's fine. See you soon."

Rachel watched as the movers pulled the ramp out of the back of their truck and once they were ready, let them inside the basement through the bulkhead.

Hannah's car swerved into the driveway next to the truck.

"Geez, Hannah. Be careful. You almost ran that guy over."

"You said get over here quick, so I was as quick as I could be. I'll start in the bedroom. Is Lucy watching Everly?"

"Yup. That's the beauty of having a sister who works from home. I better be careful though; I don't want to take advantage of her situation. One of these days she's going to tell me to find someone else."

"Highly unlikely. We're both in love with that little girl. I'll go as fast as I can. I just wanted to take one last look. I'm feeling so sad."

"I know what you mean, there are tons of memories in this place."

Hannah went through each room and piled the items she wanted in the corner of the living room.

"Where are you going to put all that?"

"I don't know. I'll figure it out later."

An hour later, the movers were done. Rachel paid the driver and then watched them drive away. Rachel figured this was as good a time as any to ask her about Oliver.

"Hannah, before you go, do you mind if I ask you about Oliver? What happened between the two of you?"

"Did he ask you to ask me?"

Deciding it was better to lie than to upset her further, Rachel shook her head.

"No. I was just wondering. He seems like a really nice guy. I can't imagine what he could have done to upset you like this."

Hannah walked to the window and looked out over the water.

"I don't think Oliver was really in love with me."

Confused, Rachel walked to her sister and placed a hand on her back. "Did he ever tell you that he was?"

Hannah nodded. "He did. He even hinted around that we might get married in time."

"I'm sorry, Hannah, but I'm not following you. If Oliver said he was in love with you, why didn't you believe him?"

Hannah turned to face Rachel.

"I did at first. I even told him I was in love with him too. Everything was perfect. I was sure we were going to get married and live happily-ever-after. That was the plan anyway."

"What changed your mind?"

"We were at his friend's wedding and when I was in the lady's room the bride was in there at the same time. We were putting our makeup on, and she turned to me and said that she couldn't get over how much I looked like Oliver's previous girlfriend."

Ever since Hannah was a little girl, she used her hands when she talked, the more excited she got the more animated she became. Now, her arms flew left and right with a few heavy sighs thrown in. Rachel did her best to remain as calm as possible for Hannah's sake as well as her own.

Hannah continued.

"She said that she was so happy for us because Oliver had such a hard time getting over Kristen. She was happy that he'd finally found someone who cared for him because he deserved to be happy."

"And?"

Hannah seemed to lose patience with her.

"Seriously, Rachel? You don't see the problem? It's obvious. He wasn't really in love with me but because I looked so much like Kristen—the woman he had a hard time getting over—he convinced himself that he loved me but it really was her he was still in love with."

As convoluted as all this sounded to Rachel, she was able to follow her sister's thinking. Although she didn't agree with Hannah, she understood her concern.

"I suppose you never talked to Oliver about this?"

"What was the point? How could he defend something he didn't even know he felt?"

Of the three sisters, Hannah was a mixture of innocence, compassion and confusion, but was so adorable it was hard to find fault in anything she did or said. However, there were limits. Rachel needed to point out to Hannah that she was in jeopardy of losing a wonderful and devoted man who clearly still loved her.

"Honey, listen to your big sister. You need to talk to Oliver. Tell him everything that happened and how it made you feel. You have to give him the opportunity to explain himself. Can't you believe that he knows his feelings better than anyone else? Don't assume anything. If you want my opinion, I think he loves you very much—you, not Kristen. Why don't you give him a chance to show it?"

There was a glimmer of hope in Hannah's eyes but Rachel could tell her sister wasn't giving in that quickly.

"I don't know. Do you really think I should?"

"I do."

"What if he's changed his mind? What if he decides I'm too high maintenance?"

It was a good question but having the benefit of seeing Oliver's face when he talked about Hannah, Rachel wasn't worried at all.

"I have a strong feeling that's not an issue. Even if he's on the fence, I think it's important for you to say what you want. Don't leave everything to Oliver. It's not like you should be waiting to see if he wants you or not. Do you want to be with him?"

Hannah nodded her head.

"I really do, Rachel. I'm just scared. I think I was so scared when that woman told me about Kristen, I freaked and ran away. I don't like confrontation and will do anything to avoid it."

"Like breaking up with Oliver?"

"I figured if I left him first, he wouldn't get the chance to leave me."

Rachel hugged Hannah and then pushed a strand of hair off her face and behind her ear.

"My dear, you think so little of yourself. Trust your big sister. Any man would be lucky to be loved by you."

Hannah beamed.

"You really think so? Thanks, Rachel. You're the best. Help me take this stuff out to my car?"

"You bet."

Rachel marveled at how quickly her sister could change subjects and moods.

They carried the pile of their aunt's belongings to Hannah's car, and after they dumped everything into the trunk, Hannah hugged Rachel once more.

"I'll talk to you later. I've got to get this stuff back to my place and then head over to the spa."

"Listen, I'm going to want details after you talk to Oliver so make sure you call me and tell me everything."

"I will. I promise."

Rachel decided against telling Oliver about her talk with Hannah. If she was right, by this time tomorrow, Hannah would do the talking for her. By Christmas, Oliver and Hannah would be exchanging kisses under the mistletoe once again.

Hannah laughed and drove off before Rachel could tell her not to mention their talk with Oliver. All in all she thought it went well.

You haven't lost your touch Rachel. Maybe you can have a thriving business as The Cape Cod Matchmaker.

Aunt Kathleen wasn't the type to sit in a rocking chair and watch the world go by. She refused to cut her long gray hair and wore it half up, held in place with colorful handmade combs. Although she'd never married, her aunt had a string of boyfriends when she was young. To this day, those who still lived in town shared so many loving thoughts about her.

"Your aunt and I used to go dancing every first Tuesday of the month when Periwinkle Shores held their monthly barn dance. She really knew how to cut a rug," said Forrest Michaelson.

"Kathleen made the best blueberry pie. She used to make one for me every few weeks. I think she still had a crush on me, after all these years," boasted Gregory Perry.

Rachel spent hours looking over old pictures that her aunt had painstakingly placed inside her scrapbooks. Scrapbooking was a passion of Kathleen's, along with knitting, making jewelry, baking and preserving jams and jellies.

Her aunt's garden in the back of the house provided all the fruit and vegetables she needed to enjoy even in winter. The freezer was jam-packed with frozen bags of Cape Cod cranberries. Rachel remembered her aunt's delicious Thanksgiving stuffing recipe that included the precious round fruit.

Looking around the house, it was hard to accept that Kathleen was gone. With Everly asleep, Rachel laid back on the sofa and pulled Kathleen's handmade quilt over her body. Colorful squares sewn together to make a large blanket to fit a grown man, she cuddled under the wool and thought about her next move.

The house would need more work in the spring, but for now, she could picture her first Christmas here. The holiday was only two weeks away, and she didn't have any Christmas decorations. At the very least she'd need a Christmas tree.

She sat up and looked around for her cell phone. She dialed Lucy's number and sat back against the sofa. Lucy's voice seemed fuzzy and distant.

"Hey, Rachel. What's up?"

"Did I wake you?"

"Um, yeah, something like that."

"Oh, man. I'm sorry. Wait. It's only six o'clock. Why are you sleeping?"

"Because I thought I'd watch a movie, but my eyes had other ideas."

"Oh, well, listen. I need a Christmas tree."

"Right now?"

"Well, yeah. The sooner the better. I want Everly to see lights tonight. Don't you think she'll love it?"

Lucy was still underwhelmed by Rachel's idea.

"Yeah, I'm sure she will. Tomorrow night. When you get your tree then."

Rachel had always been able to make pouting sounds just pathetic enough to convince Lucy to do what she wanted.

"Aw...Come on... It's for your niece. Your one and only niece and her first Christmas."

Lucy yawned.

"Fine. I'll be right over."

Rachel held Everly in her arms and looked around the Christmas tree lot. Light snow fell on the trees, giving them a delicate coating of white. People smiled and waved at Everly, with an occasional tug of her tiny boots.

Lucy touch Everly's nose with hers and moved it back and forth, making the child giggle with every attempt.

"Rachel your BBB is the cutest kid here."

"BBB?"

"Yeah, 'Bundled-Beyond-Belief.' Don't you think you've gone a bit overboard with the outer clothing for her?"

"You think it's too much?"

"Yes, I do. She's not going to turn into a frozen statue. I'm surprised she can breathe in that getup."

Rachel sighed. "I wonder how long it's going to take me to learn everything about being a good mother?"

Lucy laughed. "Last I heard, it's a lifetime, and even then you still feel like you've screwed up. Don't worry, you're in good company, every mother feels the way you do. Just do the best you can."

Lucy sighed.

"Let's start by pulling this scarf out from under this child's coat."

As Lucy undid Everly's one-piece jacket, Rachel stood frozen in place, and not because of the cold.

"I can't believe it."

"What?" Lucy asked.

"Jack Harris. He works here too?"

"Rachel, I already told you, Jack does a million things in this town. I'm not at all surprised he's here. Why? What's the problem?"

Rachel shook her head.

"The guy gets on my nerves that's all."

Just then, Jack waved and walked toward them.

"Hey, Lucy. Hello again, Rachel."

He reached down and touched Everly's cheek."

"This must be Everly. She's adorable."

Rachel smiled and did her best to be polite.

"Thank you."

"So, are you ladies here to pick out a Christmas tree?"

Great. He's clearly a genius. Why else would we be standing in a Christmas tree lot?

Lucy responded.

"Yup. It's Everly's first Christmas so we want the best tree you've got."

Jack nodded and turned.

"Follow me."

They walked to the far end of the lot.

"These are the best Balsam Firs on the lot. Aren't they gorgeous?"

Rachel shook her head.

"Too tall for the living room."

When Lucy disagreed, Rachel corrected her sister.

"It's a cottage, remember?"

Jack interrupted. "That's true, your place doesn't have tall ceilings, but I can cut the bottom as much as you'd like. The symmetry of the branches still make these trees the most desirable."

She stared at him.

"Aren't these trees more money than the shorter ones? Why would I pay more money to have you cut it to the size of the cheaper ones?"

No one said a word, and Rachel continued to glare at him.

Lucy looked mortified and Rachel could feel her sister's tug at her coat sleeve.

Jack answered Rachel.

"Yes, they are more money, but because this is Everly's first Christmas, we'll only charge you the cheaper price. How does that sound?"

It sounds as if I've now had two encounters with this man and both times he's done me a favor. Not the best way to begin a relationship with someone she planned to ignore.

Rachel couldn't stand the thought of being indebted to him once again, so she turned and walked to the shorter trees.

"No, thank you just the same, but I prefer one of these trees."

Lucy looked like she was going to lose it right where she stood.

Jack just smiled and nodded his head.

"I'll get one of the guys to get the tree ready. That will be forty dollars."

As Rachel handed him the money, Lucy smiled, trying to salvage whatever goodwill she could.

"Thank you, Jack. It was nice to see you again. I hope you and your family have a lovely Christmas."

Jack smiled at Lucy and bowed.

"And to you, Lucy, and your family as well."

He turned to Rachel and Everly and tugged at the child's boot once again.

"See you soon, Everly." And with that, he turned and walked away.

CHAPTER 5

*T*here wasn't much Hannah could do except be honest. No matter how silly the whole thing was to anyone else, her concerns about Oliver's sincerity were real and no one could tell her otherwise. She'd have to hear the truth from Oliver's lips before she would admit her feelings for him.

She thought about calling him on the phone, but that wouldn't work solely for the reason that she needed to see his face. Hannah would know right away if Oliver was telling the truth. Instead, she looked for him at the favorite local hangout, *The Pearl*.

It was a Thursday night, and everyone went to *The Pearl* for drinks after work and live music. Anyone else would have found a quiet, private location to bear one's soul, but not Hannah. She knew that Oliver couldn't hide his feelings with their friends all around them. However, what she didn't count on was the noise drowning out her deepest feelings.

"I'm so glad to see you," Oliver yelled out across the table.

"What?"

"I said, I'm so glad to see you again."

Oliver grabbed Hannah's hand and pulled her outside in front of the bar.

"I'm sorry, but I couldn't hear myself think in there."

Hannah laughed at how comical they must have looked to everyone inside. She nodded and smiled.

"I don't know what I was thinking coming here, but I wanted to talk to you."

Oliver looked surprised.

"You wanted to talk to me?"

Hannah nodded.

"Yeah, I know things didn't end well and I needed to explain the reason. I'm only sorry I waited so long to talk to you about this."

Oliver moved closer to her and seemed genuinely happy to see her.

"Let's walk over to that table under the tree. It's more private."

They walked to the table and sat across from each other.

Hannah did her best to explain her concerns to Oliver and when she finished explaining what happened at his friend's wedding, she took a breath and waited for his response.

"You're telling me that you broke up with me because Jeff's wife thought you looked like Kristen?"

The question sounded awful coming from Rachel the other day, but now, hearing Oliver ask it seemed even more ridiculous.

"Hannah, have you ever seen what Kristen looks like?"

She had no choice but to lie. It would sound terrible if she'd told the truth that she had checked Kristen out online. The last thing she needed Oliver to think was that she was a cyberstalker.

Instead she shook her head.

"Her last name is Crenshaw. We're still friends on Facebook if you want to see what she looks like. I'd say the only thing the two of you have in common is that you've both have blond hair. Other than that, I have no idea why Jen said that to you. It's no matter though, you should have come to me right away with your concerns."

"I agree. I should have, but sometimes people do things out of fear, and in this case, that's exactly what happened with me."

"You were afraid that I wasn't really in love with you so you did the very thing you were worried would happen to us? What you're really saying is that you didn't trust me to be honest with you. Is that how you felt? Is it how you feel now?"

His words danced around her head, spinning her perspective and making her feel more vulnerable than ever.

"You're right. I messed up big time, but I do trust you. I let my insecurities get the better of me and ran away instead of talking to you about my fears. Do you think you might forgive me for being so stupid?"

Oliver shook his head.

"You're hardly stupid, Hannah. I take responsibility for not telling you how much you meant to me back then. I thought I had, but maybe I wasn't clear enough. I don't want to make that mistake again. If you'll let me, I'd like to get another chance to show you just how much you do mean to me. In case you didn't realize it, I'm in love with you. I've been in love with you for months now. As beautiful as you are on the outside, I love what's inside more. I love your heart. It would be impossible for Kristen or any other woman to capture mine. Any chance you might feel the same?"

Having a large crowd of people around made it difficult to show him how happy she was, so Hannah said the words she'd been holding onto for weeks.

"I'm in love with you too."

Hannah loved that Oliver didn't seem to care that many of their friends would see them kissing. He didn't hold back as he pulled Hannah into his arms and kissed her, leaving nothing to chance ever again.

Talking to Oliver about her concerns was the best decision Hannah had made in a long time. She took Rachel's advice and it paid off. She felt the weight of the world fall off her shoulders and she had her sister to thank for that.

Maybe now is the right time to come clean about the spa's financial troubles. Rachel might know what I should do.

On the drive to Rachel's house, Hannah practiced what she would say to her sister. It was embarrassing to admit that although she enjoyed having her own business, she didn't have the skills to make it a success. Numbers always eluded her and she worried she might have to close the spa for good if business didn't pick up.

"Hannah, I was just going to call you. Did you have a chance to talk to Oliver?"

Hannah hugged Rachel and walked into the living room. Clapping her hands in excitement she walked over to the newly installed Christmas tree.

"Oh, Rachel, It's beautiful. When did you get it?"

Laughing, Rachel said, "I can't believe you think it's beautiful. It doesn't have one decoration on it. Right now it's just a tree. Anyway, I got it last night. I called Lucy and she helped Everly and me pick it out. Everly isn't really sure what a tree is doing inside the house, but she'll be more excited about it once we get lights on it."

"Is she asleep?"

"Yes, I finally got her to settle down. She's one of those babies who fears missing out on stuff, so it takes a while for her to succumb. So, tell me about Oliver."

Hannah turned and as she began to explain everything to Rachel, her arms flew up in the air and waved left to right as she spoke.

"It was incredible, Rachel. It happened just the way you said it would. I should have talked to him long ago about it. I've been so stupid and made a big deal out of nothing."

"I take it that means the two of you are back together?"

Hannah hugged Rachel again.

"Yes, and I have you to thank for that. Thank you so much for giving me advice."

Lucy opened the front door and joined them in the living room.

"Hey, Rachel, I stopped by Target and got you a bunch of lights for the tree. Hannah, I didn't know you were coming over."

Rachel looked at Hannah for permission to talk about Oliver.

Hannah nodded and her faced beamed with joy.

"It seems that Hannah and Oliver have made up and are back together."

'No kidding? That's great. I really like Oliver. I should have guessed since Hannah's face looks like she's covered in Christmas lights."

Hannah laughed. "I've never been very good at keeping my emotions inside. Speaking of emotions and stuff…"

Hannah paused and waited for courage to emerge. She had felt strong and determined only an hour ago, but now, in front of both her sisters, she was terrified of their reaction.

"Guys, I'm in trouble. I really need advice on what to do. The spa is going to close down if it doesn't make more money. Right now, my expenses are surpassing my income. I've tried to make sense of the numbers, but I've never been very good at it, and now, when I do the math, it looks like I don't have any other choice but to close."

Hannah plopped down onto the sofa, dejected and overcome with sadness. She was amazed at the roller coaster of emotions she had experienced in the last two hours.

Rachel sat next to Hannah and put her hand on her sister's back.

"Honey, how long has this been going on?"

CHRISTMAS ON THE CAPE

"It's been months now. I've been living on the savings I had in the bank and now that amount is slowly going down by the spa's expenses. Soon, I won't have anything."

She bent down and put her face in her hands. Holding back tears, she took a deep breath and waited for Lucy and Rachel to shed some light on the problem.

Lucy joined them on the sofa.

"Hannah, why didn't you come to us sooner?"

Hannah looked up at Lucy.

"How could I? Rachel's had her own problems lately and you're so busy with your writing deadlines, I never wanted to bother either of you with this. The only reason I'm telling you now is I'm at my wits end. There's not much left to do but the obvious."

Rachel looked at Lucy who shrugged her shoulders. Hannah could tell this was one problem not so easily remedied by her sisters.

"Honey, I know I've had a lot on my plate after Everly was born, but nothing is more important than family. The three of us is all we've got since Dad has basically been unavailable to us since he married Melanie. We're got to make a promise to each other that no matter what's going on, we need to stay close. Agreed?"

"Agreed." Lucy answered

With tears in her eyes, Hannah nodded. "Agreed."

"Ok, now that that's out of the way, the first thing I think we should do is have a look at your books. Maybe things aren't as bad as you think. I'm not saying they aren't, but until I get in there and look over the numbers, let's not panic. Actually, no matter what the situation is, we shouldn't panic. Surely, the three of us will be able to come up with a solution."

"Rachel's right, Hannah. There are three of us now. We've got this."

Hannah felt much better for talking with her sisters. The day had been a success, even if no final decision had been made on her business. For now, she allowed herself a moment of gratitude. She and Oliver had found their way back to each other. No matter what lay ahead for *The Pink Seashell,* she had people in her life who loved her and would always be there for her. That was worth celebrating.

"How about we have a glass of wine? We need to toast to the good news about you and Oliver."

Hannah nodded. "That sounds good to me."

Lucy agreed and Rachel went into the kitchen to get the wine.

"I really hope I don't have to close the spa. It's the only way I get all the Periwinkle Shores gossip. Sometimes I get Wellfleet gossip too. Come to think of it, I probably get all the news from Eastham to Provincetown especially when Selma Warner comes in."

"Who's Selma Warner?" Rachel asked.

"Only the biggest mouth in three counties. You remember Selma. She graduated with you," Lucy said.

"I swear I don't remember anyone. Apparently Jack Harris graduated with me too. At least that's what he said when he did my plumbing."

Hannah's arms flailed in the air once again.

"Oh my goodness, Rachel, that's who Selma talks about all the time. She tells everyone that they're a couple, but the truth is that only Selma thinks they are. I think Jack doesn't want to be rude, but I'm pretty sure he wants nothing to do with her."

Lucy chimed in as well.

"No one wants anything to do with Selma. She's a pain in the…"

"Lucy. Be kind," Rachel said.

"Seriously, Rachel, I know what I'm talking about. Poor Jack has been taking care of his father for as long as I can remember. His mother passed away a few years ago, and Jack's left to take care of everything, including trying to run the vineyard, although

I hear he's been having a hard time getting help lately. To be honest, there isn't a woman in Periwinkle Shores who isn't crazy about the guy. He's never been married, incredibly handsome, and has a wonderful sense of humor. He's a real catch. Anyway, he doesn't need Selma's insinuations."

There was plenty about Jack Harris that Rachel couldn't understand, but she didn't allow herself to think more about him. Instead, she carried the wine glasses into the living room and handed them to Hannah and Lucy. Raising her glass she looked at Hannah.

"To Hannah and Oliver. May they have many more years together, and maybe soon we'll be attending their wedding."

Hannah blushed. She didn't want to admit it to her sisters, at least not today, but she'd been privately praying for that very thing.

Rachel turned to Lucy and smiled.

"And to our sister, Lucy. May she finally find Mr. Wonderful and follow in our sister Hannah's footsteps."

Lucy didn't drink her wine after Rachel's statement, but instead put her glass down on the table and looked upset.

Hannah rolled her eyes, knowing something Rachel didn't. That Lucy had little interest in falling in love and was perfectly content with writing about happily-ever-after instead of living it for real.

CHAPTER 6

*R*achel waved to Hannah and then pushed the front door against the roaring wind coming off the water.

"That wind is keeping the temperature about ten degrees colder than the forecaster says it is."

Lucy laughed. "I bet you wouldn't have moved here if you thought it was going to be like this."

"I thought it was supposed to be warmer near the water. I was looking forward to that fact when I moved here."

"Yeah, I don't believe anything they say about the weather. This is New England after all. You and I both know whatever it is, just wait a few minutes and it will change. I guess you could say us New Englanders can depend on the undependable."

Rachel filled her glass with a bit more wine.

"Do you want any more?"

"No. Hannah and I are such lightweights, which is a blessing I guess. I don't want to get stopped for drinking and driving."

Lucy got up and looked at the dark wood hutch in the corner.

"I see you've kept all of Aunt Kathleen's knick knacks. I call them 'something to dust' myself."

Carrying her wine, Rachel joined Lucy. She opened the

cabinet and looked over their aunt's collection of Hummels, Herend and Lladro figurines. Ainsley china teacups, Baccarat and Waterford crystal wine glasses adorned a mirrored shelf.

Rachel ran her finger over the crystal.

"I remember Aunt Kathleen's formal dinners. Do you remember when we had to get dressed up and pretend we were royalty?"

Lucy smiled and shrugged.

"Barely. The weird thing is how strange it was to see three girls that were nowhere near close in age. I mean, think about that. When you were seventeen, I was five years old. Hannah wasn't even born yet. What could our parents have been thinking to have three children so many years apart? It couldn't have been planned."

Rachel laughed at that.

"Planned? Uh, no. I wouldn't say that."

Lucy looked somber.

"Mom and Dad started not liking each other when Hannah was around ten, but I don't really remember a happy childhood."

Rachel frowned.

"You don't? I do. Don't you remember all the parties and lobster bakes that we had?"

Lucy shrugged.

"You weren't around when I was a teenager. You were long gone by then, and Hannah barely remembers seeing you except for the occasional visits you made to the Cape."

Rachel could hear the pain in Lucy's voice and felt guilty for being absent in her life.

"I'm not complaining, Rachel. I would have done the same thing you did back then. You couldn't stay around here just for Hannah and me."

The look on Lucy's face did little to convince Rachel that her little sister was over the trauma of the past.

"Rachel, honestly, we can't dwell on that stuff. You're here now, and the three of us are closer than we've ever been. Isn't that enough?"

"You're right, Lucy. I'm sorry. Let's leave that stuff in the past where it belongs."

Rachel opened one of the drawers and looked inside. She could see something in the back of the drawer but couldn't reach it.

"There's something in the back. I can't get to it though. Let me use the flashlight on your cell phone."

Bending down, Lucy pointed the light toward the back of the drawer.

"It looks like something wrapped with a piece of rope. Maybe get a spatula or something long enough from the kitchen."

Rummaging through the kitchen drawers, Rachel found long silver tongs and handed them to Lucy.

"Perfect. Let me try."

Lucy clasped the tongs onto the package and pulled. It took two attempts before the object moved forward and they could see the stack of letters wrapped with elastic covered with a tan-colored thin rope.

Rachel grabbed the letters and the two women sat on the sofa.

She removed the rope and elastic and loosened the pile onto the coffee table.

"That's strange. These are all addressed to Aunt Kathleen, but there isn't a return address on the envelopes."

Lucy seemed to lose patience and grabbed one letter off the table. Opening it, a photograph fell out onto the floor. Rachel picked it up.

"Hey, there's Aunt Kathleen, but I have no idea who the guy is."

There were four more photos in the envelope and other than their aunt, Rachel didn't have a clue who the other people in the photo were.

"Oh my goodness, Lucy. Do you know where this is?"

Lucy shook her head.

"It's Woodstock. I can tell. Look at the way everyone is dressed and the face paint. It's definitely Woodstock. Wait."

Rachel pointed to a man who was in three of the four photos.

"This guy. He looks familiar. I swear I've seen him before. Maybe he lives in town."

She looked at the last page for a name.

"I think the guy in the pictures is the one who wrote this letter. Listen to this."

Dearest Kathleen,

I'm never going to forget our time together. Showing you these pictures should prove to you that I've never forgotten what we had. No matter what has happened between us, you have always been the only woman I've truly loved. I'm sorry that our lives took different paths. It was all because of my stupidity that we couldn't be together. What does a man do when he regrets his entire life? My choice cost us a beautiful life together. So many years have passed, and what's done is done, but I still need you to know that you've always been the one...the only one... who has had my heart. Please forgive me.

Yours forever,

Martin.

Rachel looked at Lucy.

"Did Aunt Kathleen ever say anything to you about someone named Martin?"

Lucy shook her head.

"Nope. We talked about what life was like when she was younger and everyone in town knows there were several guys interested in her, even at her age. I bet it's someone from another town."

Rachel's mouth opened and she put her hand to it.

"Oh it can't be."

"What? What can't be?"

"Martin Harris is Jack Harris's father. Give me those pictures."

Rachel looked at the photos again.

"That's got to be him. I'm not really sure what he looks like but I bet it's him. Jack mentioned something about his father to me the day he did the plumbing here. It's hard to tell since the picture was taken in 1969. He's got to be about seventy-two now but I swear that's him. That's incredible. Aunt Kathleen and Martin Harris. Oh, this is too good."

Lucy stuffed the photos and letter back inside the envelope. She gathered the letters and wrapped the elastic around them.

Rachel pulled the letters away from Lucy, and then Lucy pulled them back.

"What are you doing?"

"I'm putting these away somewhere for safe keeping and then we're going to forget about them."

"What? Why?"

"Because it's private. It feels wrong to read them."

"Oh, Lucy, that's ridiculous. These belonged to our aunt. Aren't you curious about her life? This is a side of her we don't know about. I, for one, want to know more."

Rachel could see that Lucy wouldn't explain to her why reading letters from Jack's father to their aunt made her feel uncomfortable. It was obvious that Lucy refused to listen to Rachel's opinion on the matter.

"I'm putting these away somewhere safe but not in the hutch. I don't want us to delve into Aunt Kathleen's private past. Let these letters rest. Promise me you'll leave them be."

Confused, Rachel could see Lucy's internal struggle over the letters but chose to respect her sister's request. She was surprised that Lucy felt so strongly about Kathleen's privacy. If she had any doubt about it, Lucy's next words convinced Rachel to close the door on this subject.

"If Aunt Kathleen wanted them shared, she wouldn't have hidden them. She clearly was in love with Martin Harris. If she wasn't, she would have destroyed these letters or thrown them away as soon as they landed in her mailbox. For whatever reason, they couldn't be together, but holding onto his words must have represented her love for him as much as his love for her. I think it's sweet."

Rachel didn't want to think about such things. She couldn't allow herself to suppose anything about romance. Being in love with someone had changed her and not for the better. Whatever held her back from allowing the romantic life of her aunt to be anything but trouble she didn't know, but no amount of prying would help.

If anything, believing in love again, for Rachel seemed like a waste of time. She'd already lost years to the myth. Nothing in the letters of Martin Harris would prove to be more than fantasy, and she'd had enough of that already.

The letters were placed in a shoebox and Rachel carried them to the attic where she put the box inside a plastic tote. When she returned to the living room, Lucy was looking at her cell phone.

"I should probably get back home. I've got a few things to do before bed. Thanks for the wine."

Rachel stopped Lucy before she reached the front door.

"Lucy, wait. I wanted to ask you something. I noticed you didn't like my toast earlier."

"Which one?"

"Don't be coy. You know which one. What did I say that was so wrong?"

Lucy sighed.

"You didn't say anything wrong. The problem is society as a whole. I don't like the pressure to marry and have kids. That stuff isn't for everyone you know."

"I know that. I didn't mean anything by it. I just want you to be happy. Whatever that looks like for you is fine with me."

Lucy hugged Rachel.

"I know you didn't mean anything by it. I think everyone assumes that because I write romantic fiction, then I must have a romance myself. The truth is I think my standards are too high. I've set the bar quite high with my fictional men. Makes it hard to find anyone so perfect."

"Are you telling me that you make the men in your stories be perfect? How boring is that?"

Lucy laughed.

"It's not just that, Rachel. No offense to you, but look what happened in your marriage, and look at how miserable Hannah was when she and Oliver weren't speaking. I think relationships cloud a person's brain. Men get in the way of a woman's desire for independent thinking. I like being on my own without a man to deal with."

Rachel smiled and then hugged Lucy.

"You know, Lucy, before we found those letters, I would have said that you and Aunt Kathleen were two peas in a pod, content to live without romance. To be honest, I couldn't understand why she left this house to me instead of you. You and she are so alike it's scary. But now, after reading Martin's letter I'm not so sure she didn't have a love after all. Unrequited love is so sad. I hate to think that Aunt Kathleen lived her life disappointed in her choices."

Lucy shook her head.

"Aunt Kathleen lived life to the fullest. I don't think she sacrificed anything. She chose her life, just as I've chosen mine."

Rachel put her hands on Lucy's shoulders.

"She might have chosen a life without a man but we don't know the reason why she did that. You and Aunt Kathleen have more in common than you realize. The two of you have been content to experience romance and love from words on pieces of paper. Think of how much you miss living that way. Let's face it, no one is more cynical about romance and love than I am, but even I don't want you to miss out on the possibility of what it could be."

Lucy opened the front door and turned back to look at Rachel.

"Romance maybe, but never love…never love."

Rachel had no idea what her sister meant by those words, but she felt certain that just like their aunt, Lucy held much in her heart that she was unwilling to share with anyone… even her family.

CHAPTER 7

*R*achel rubbed her forehead and sighed. Hannah's bookkeeping left much to the imagination. Rachel was at a loss to figure out how bad things were for the spa, but Hannah was right. There was more money going out than was coming in.

She got up and poured herself another cup of coffee, hoping the caffeine would clear the fog from her brain. A knock at the door interrupted her calculations.

"Door's open."

Hannah peeked around the door and whispered.

"Am I disturbing you?"

Hannah had found three different reasons within the last thirty minutes to enter the office with a lame excuse. Rachel knew it was Hannah's impatience that made it impossible for her to wait to hear Rachel's perspective on the spa's financial health.

"Hannah, why don't you just come in and sit down. I'm almost done anyway."

Rachel smiled as she watched Hannah bounce into the room and pull up a chair next to her.

"Well?"

"Well, what I see is that you either have to get more customers or you have to reduce your expenses. You're right in thinking that you'll have to close down if things continue this way. What about this expense here—Fashionable Fragrance?"

"Oh, I need that. I mix it with the hand lotion we use."

"Can't you use the hand lotion without the fragrance?"

"Well, I could, but it wouldn't smell as nice."

"What about this one—Jenny's Jelly?"

"That's what we use to wax our clients. It's really the best on the market."

"Are there cheaper version of this wax?"

"Of course."

"Then why not buy that instead?"

Hannah rolled her eyes. "Seriously, Rachel. I can tell you don't know much about waxes. Some of the stuff out there is terrible for the skin."

"Uh-huh. Hannah, do you understand what I'm talking about when I say reduce your expenses? I don't think you do. This is a sink or swim situation. Your best bet is to reduce your expenses AND get more clients. I'm afraid without both of those things, you'll need to close *The Pink Seashell*."

Hannah looked defeated.

"I've tried both things, Rachel. I'm not very good at running a business."

"Stop that! I don't want to hear you talk about yourself that way. You're not the first person to close shop and you won't be the last. If there is any way to keep the spa open, we'll do it. Let me see if any of my friends up north are coming down for the Christmas Stroll. If they are, we'll get them booked in here for a pampering day. I'll ask around and tell Lucy to get the word out too. It's at least worth trying before you close the doors on *The Pink Seashell*."

Hannah smiled and hugged Rachel.

"Thank you so much. You're the best sister in the world, well you and Lucy are."

"Ok. Now that we have a plan, how about you go out front and get back to work? Oh, one more thing."

Rachel held up a Christmas themed flyer for the spa.

"What do you think? Lucy and I are going to go around town and see if we can put these in store front windows."

Hannah clapped.

"Oh, I love it. Did you make that?"

"I did. I used something called Canva on the computer. Took me about thirty minutes to create."

Rachel was happy to see that she'd helped Hannah feel better about everything. Even though she couldn't promise a miracle, she'd pray for one anyway.

They placed flyers all over town and Lucy even drove up and down Rte. 6 to find new customers for *The Pink Seashell.* After several days of running around with their flyers, Hannah reported that she'd had five new clients. She was thrilled but knew that the numbers were still much less than she needed to keep the place open.

When the day of the Christmas Stroll came around, the women held little hope for Hannah's business. The best they could do was to forget about their troubles for a few days, just long enough to celebrate the holiday with Everly.

Rachel looked forward to celebrating with townspeople she hadn't seen in years. She had fond memories of the Stroll and remembered a time when her family helped to decorate the town's Christmas tree.

She couldn't wait to see Everly's reaction to the colorful lights. Christmas music was played by local musicians staged under the large white gazebo and carolers dressed in period costume walked along the town green which was covered in snow.

Rachel smiled and said hello to many who passed her on the sidewalk. Several women from her high school graduating class welcomed her and Everly back to Periwinkle Shores.

"Rachel Adams, I can't believe it's you. How have you been?"

Sherry Turner and Brenda Flaherty reminded Rachel of why she hated high school so much. Back when they were kids, both women were friendly to your face, but gossiped about you behind your back. Now, they stood before Rachel pretending the three of them had always been best friends.

"Oh, I'm fine, thanks. You both look just like you did back in high school."

Rachel figured a small fib couldn't hurt.

The women giggled and rolled their eyes.

"Go on! You are so sweet. My goodness, is this your little girl?"

"Yup. This is my daughter Everly."

Sherry wiggled Everly's shoes.

"Hello, sweetie. I'm Sherry and this is Brenda, and you are adorable."

Pointing to three children standing next to Brenda.

"That's Michael, Michaela, and Michelle. They're mine. Brenda has two but they're home right now with colds."

Rachel wanted to get away from the women but didn't have a clue how to walk away without seeming impolite. As if he knew what she was thinking, Jack Harris appeared out of nowhere beside Rachel and nodded hello to Sherry and Brenda.

"Rachel, didn't you say you needed to find Lucy? I found her down near Santa's Workshop. I told her I'd go find you and Everly."

Rachel smiled at Jack.

"Oh, great. Well, ladies, it was nice to see you again. I've got to find my sister. You all have a wonderful Christmas. Take care."

Jack placed his hand under Rachel's elbow and escorted her away from the women. Sherry and Brenda waved and then turned to each other in what Rachel could only imagine was gossip about her and Jack getting cozy.

"Thanks for that, although I'm not sure I like what they're thinking."

Jack smiled.

"I do."

They didn't say another word until they were on the far side of the festivities. Rachel stopped and looked up at Jack.

"Why do you keep doing that?"

"What am I doing?"

"You keep rescuing me."

"I thought you needed rescuing. Didn't you want me to rescue you?"

"Yes, I mean no. I mean…"

"You seem to have a hard time knowing what you want. Do I make you nervous or something?"

Rachel was losing patience with him, but more than that she didn't want him to walk away thinking she was always so rude.

"No. You don't make me nervous. It's just that I'm not used to people doing things for me, and you've done enough already."

Just then, Lucy waved and walked toward them.

"Hey, I'm glad I found you. Santa Claus is taking requests for gifts. I don't think Everly has any just yet, but I bet she'd love to get her picture taken with Santa."

Lucy took Everly in her arms.

"Thanks, Lucy."

"Aww it's fine. I've been waiting to spoil this little cherub all night. See you two in a bit."

Lucy and Everly made their way to Santa. Rachel felt awkward standing before Jack without the baby in her arms.

Somehow Everly had felt like a protective barrier between the two of them and now she felt vulnerable and unsure of what to do with her hands.

Without direction they walked through the crowd of carolers and shoppers. A light snow fell around them. It took a few minutes before anyone said a word. Rachel cleared her throat and then said the first thing that came into her head.

"I understand that your family owns Stellar Seas Vineyard. I've driven by that place for years but never went in. Well, only once before I was old enough to drink. I was with friends and we spent most of the time in there giggling and trying to figure out which one of us would go up to the register to ask for a bottle of wine."

"Did it work?"

"We never got the guts to do it. I suspect we would have been thrown out of the place for trying. You know teenagers."

Jack smiled and nodded. "Yes, I was one once."

Rachel laughed. "Of course."

"The vineyard means a lot to me, but it's a full time job and I've got lots of other things I'm involved in as well. It would be easier if we had more help, but no one wants to work anymore. Plus, being on the Cape, we don't always get people who want to be here for work. They'd rather be at the beach or at one of the clubs in the summer months," he explained.

"So it's just you and your father, right?"

"Not exactly. It takes more than two people to run a vineyard. I assume someone told you about my mother dying?"

"Yes, Lucy mentioned it. I'm sorry."

Jack shook his head.

"It's been interesting. My parents weren't the type to show lots of affection. I'm not even sure they liked each other. But, whatever their feelings, they stayed together for almost forty years, so that's something I guess."

Rachel thought about the letters from Jack's father to her aunt

Kathleen. To hear Jack tell it, his parents weren't in love. It explained only part of the story. Rachel suddenly wished she'd read the rest of her aunt's letters.

"I'm sorry to hear that. Marriage is hard enough when two people love each other."

The way Jack looked at her she realized that he must have thought she was talking about her marriage and subsequent divorce. She felt embarrassed and needed to change the subject. Fortunately, Lucy and Everly found them. Everly was crying.

"What happened?"

"I think Santa was too scary for her. Her eyes were wide and she seemed mesmerized by him at first. The minute I put her on his lap, it was all over. She screamed and then cried. She's been crying ever since."

Rachel started to reach for Everly, but Jack stopped her.

"Let me try. I'm pretty good at this."

Jack gingerly took Everly in his arms, and she immediately stopped crying. Instead, she stuck her finger in her mouth as she looked into his eyes. He walked toward the giant snow globe and pointed at the falling snow inside. Everly put her hand on the plastic bubble and Jack did the same. Together they looked like they were having a private party all their own.

Lucy looked at Rachel and smiled.

"Looks like you've got yourself a new babysitter."

Rachel wasn't so sure. Jack Harris had woven his life into hers and he'd done it so effortlessly that it seemed like he'd been part of her family forever. She didn't know what to make of it, but she knew she didn't like it. Before it got out of hand, she decided to take Everly from him, and find her way back to her house.

She reached for Everly and thanked Jack.

"I think she's just tired. It's been a busy day. Time to head back home."

"Can I give you ladies a ride? It's pretty cold out."

Rachel shook her head.

"Nope. We're good. It's only a few blocks away. Thank you."

She'd walked so fast away from him, Lucy barely whispered goodbye to him. While Rachel faced forward, Lucy turned and waved goodbye to Jack, and Everly kept her eyes on him until they turned the corner and she couldn't see him anymore.

CHAPTER 8

$\mathcal{L}$ucy didn't care what people thought of her. Just like her Rachel, she had uncontrollable brown hair. Thick, coarse hair ran on her mother's side and it was one of the things Lucy loved most about her Aunt Kathleen.

In Hannah's case, she'd mastered how to tame her blond curls into larger intentional waves. Rachel's hair was a little shorter than Lucy's, and often wore a bandana headband to keep the strands off her face. That along with the jade drop earrings that matched her eyes, gave Rachel a bohemian look.

Lucy envied Rachel's porcelain skin and spent lots of money over the years trying to match what nature gave her sister.

She'd had many hours of private time with her aunt, and of the three sisters, Lucy was the one who struggled the most with Kathleen's death.

A loner, Lucy thought of Kathleen not just as her aunt, but as a mentor. To Lucy, Kathleen represented everything a woman should be. Free and without the need to answer to anyone seemed more powerful than any other life she could imagine. Her aunt lived her life on her terms, and there was never a time when Lucy felt that Kathleen had regrets for her choices.

"Autonomy is everything, Lucy. Mark my words, you shouldn't depend on anyone to show up on your doorstep with all the answers. You're going to have to find out for yourself what you want out of life. First, you must know who you are, and once you do, make no apologies for it."

Kathleen's words danced in her mind constantly, and she wrote down every single thing her aunt told her about life and how to overcome obstacles.

Often, Lucy felt confused by her feelings. She'd given them power when she acknowledged them, but when she questioned why she felt the way she did, only more questions would arise. Introspection was not something her family did. Rather they were content to let someone else be in control, but not Kathleen.

"Don't be afraid to speak up. If you feel that something is wrong, say so. Your voice is the most powerful thing you own. Don't let anyone take it from you. I'm not just talking about men either. Don't let anyone— man or woman— silence you."

Lucy took her aunt's words to heart and lived her life proudly and as authentically as she knew how. Whenever she had questions, she'd look to her aunt for answers. True to her nature, Aunt Kathleen would ask more questions than give answers. In the end, Lucy would find the answers herself, which was what her aunt had intended all along.

When Kathleen died, Lucy felt like a piece of her died as well. She couldn't accept that she'd never hear her aunt's voice ever again. To say she fell into a depression was one way to describe her behavior.

She was also more likely to lash out at anyone who she disagreed with. Rachel's coming home helped Lucy calm down a bit, and she was once again welcomed inside the local establishments that had thrown her out for fighting with other customers.

The strongest of the three women, Lucy wasn't afraid of much. When her sister Rachel finally confided in her about how terrible her marriage to Brian was and how much abuse she had experienced, it was Lucy who vowed to protect her big sister from anyone who tried to hurt her ever again. She'd switched roles and for a while was the big sister when Rachel could barely get out of bed.

Rachel always said that Lucy was a combination of the character of Idgie Threadgoode from the movie *Fried Green Tomatoes* and Helena Bonham Carter's character in the movie *Howard's End*. Both characters weren't afraid of anything, and both kept secrets. From the moment she was born, her older sister, Rachel would often ask, "What secrets is Lucy hiding from us all? She knows things she's not telling."

Her aunt's secrets didn't go to the grave with Kathleen. Instead, Lucy knew every detail of Kathleen's hopes and dreams. She shared them with her niece at odd times. First thing in the morning, when Kathleen would show up outside Lucy's bedroom window ringing a cow bell and telling Lucy to hurry up because she had to show her something.

Or the time when Lucy walked in on her aunt dancing to Janis Joplin music and insisted Lucy join in.

Kathleen talked about Woodstock and how much better the world was back then. She made being a hippie sound attractive, so Lucy started wearing a suede fringed jacket with peace and love symbols written all over it in blue ink.

They'd dance to the music of a time that Lucy could only imagine but would sit with her aunt and listen to stories that she held close to her heart.

There wasn't much Kathleen left unsaid, even when it came to Martin Harris. Lucy saw her time with her aunt as sacred, so whatever was said between them, she'd promised her aunt to keep it all to herself. The memories were hers, and the stories belonged to her as well.

Even now that Kathleen was gone, Lucy knew she could tell her sisters about their aunt's life, but she refused to do so. Lucy couldn't share what she knew with anyone. To do so would mean that her aunt was really gone forever, a truth she wasn't ready to accept.

Christine agreed to watch Everly for a few hours so that Rachel could do some Christmas shopping. As much as Rachel wanted to give Everly every toy she could find, she did her best to keep the amount of gifts under the tree reasonable and yet festive. She knew that Hannah and Lucy were already spoiling her daughter and tried to not set a precedent she'd have to maintain year after year.

While Rachel waited for the store clerk to wrap two large gifts, she saw Jack Harris across the street putting long pieces of lumber into the back of his truck. The amount of lumber was significant and Rachel wondered what use a plumber would have for so much wood.

The last few days she'd struggled with wanting to unravel the mystery surrounding Jack's father and her Aunt Kathleen's relationship but remembered her promise to Lucy to mind her business and let that subject rest.

However, nothing was said about her getting information from Jack on the matter. The problem was trying to find a way to talk to him without overtly mentioning her aunt.

Besides, she'd already been rude to Jack on more than one occasion. He'd get suspicious if she came right up to him and acted like they were good friends. In the end she figured the best way to get his attention was to walk by him and let things naturally occur.

With her newly wrapped gifts under her arms, she crossed the street and intentionally walked by Jack's truck. When he didn't call out to her, she was forced to continue along without acknowledging him at all.

So much for my plan. Maybe it would have worked if you hadn't been such a jerk to him.

She decided to go inside the adjacent store and kill a few minutes, all the while looking out the window to see what Jack was doing. She didn't realize that the store clerk was watching her.

"Can I help you with something?"

Flustered, Rachel shook her head.

"No, thank you. I'm just looking."

The woman smiled and gave Rachel a knowing look.

Worried Jack would drive off and she'd lose her opportunity, she walked out of the store and their eyes met.

"Hello, Jack."

He looked surprised.

"Are you talking to me?"

"Very funny. I suppose you must think poorly of me?"

He smiled and the mixture of weak knees and anger ran through her body once again. She changed tactics in the interest of gaining information from him.

"I'm sorry. I guess I must have seemed rude to you before. I think my aunt's passing and the divorce and move have been a lot in such a short amount of time. I hope you'll forgive me?"

Jack rubbed his chin and the small amount of beard that he intentionally left on his face.

"I tell you what. I'll forgive you if you go for a drive with me."

"What will I do with my car?"

"Leave it. I'll bring you back for it later."

Rachel looked around to see if anyone saw them talking and noticed the store clerk who had smiled at her earlier was looking out the window. The woman quickly moved away from view and Rachel turned to look at Jack.

"All right. Where are we going?"

"It's a surprise. Hop in."

He took her gifts and placed them on the backseat. He then walked to the passenger door and opened it for her.

She felt awkward sitting inside Jack's truck but pushed her nerves to the side in order to keep control of her senses. She'd deliberately wanted his attention, and now that she had it, she feared he'd dominate the conversation and she'd leave him without getting any information on Martin Harris.

"For a man who runs a vineyard, you seem to spend a lot of time doing everything but that."

"What makes you think I'm not running things at Stellar?"

"Well, you're a plumber and now you've got a truck full of lumber. What's that about?"

Jack didn't look at her. Instead, keeping his eyes straight ahead on the road, he smiled and answered her.

"The plumbing I do more in the winter than anything. The lumber is for the house I'm building."

This is great. A perfect opening.

"I thought you lived with your father. Don't you already have a house?"

He didn't answer her and when the truck turned the corner and into a long driveway she understood why.

Jack stopped the truck and turned it off.

"Here we are."

A home that looked like it belonged on the cover of Architectural Digest sat before her and the stunning view made her jaw drop.

The house was a modern log home with large windows in every room. Rachel marveled at the beautiful structure nestled in the snowy forest.

"This is your house?"

Jack nodded.

"Well, it's my house but not my home, at least not right now."

"Jack, this is gorgeous. Why not your home?"

Again, he didn't answer, instead taking her arm and leading her inside.

With such a large property, it seemed impossible to create a cozy feel, but Jack had accomplished it. Rachel wondered if there was a woman's touch somewhere within.

Jack took a deep breath before continuing his thought.

"I started this house a couple of years ago. It's taken me a long time because I've had many interruptions. My father has been very ill. He has stomach cancer. I've been taking care of him."

"Oh, I'm so sorry."

"He had surgery about six months ago. They took out what they could but said that there was too much cancer and they couldn't get it all. They predicted six to nine months. Looks like their predictions are coming true."

"What about chemo?"

Jack shook his head.

"He doesn't want it. At first, he seemed willing but something changed and he said no. They told him that it would only prolong his life by months. I can understand his reluctance."

"Cancer is horrible. I have a friend in Florida who's just been diagnosed with breast cancer. They caught it early though, so I'm sure she'll do chemo and radiation just to make sure it won't come back."

They were quiet for a few minutes and the soft sound of falling snow made for an almost perfect moment. Talk of cancer never made anyone comfortable and this time was no exception. Rachel changed the subject.

"It's amazing what you've accomplished with this property. I imagine it's been helpful keeping yourself busy and your mind occupied."

"To be honest with you I've considered selling this place when I'm done with it. I picked up the lumber this morning because I'm doing some work on a shed out back. After I drop this batch off,

I'm calling it quits until spring. With the vineyard and my father, there's just too much going on right now."

Rachel suddenly felt wrong for wanting to pry into his father's affairs. She felt terrible for Jack's situation and also for the way she had treated him since she'd returned back to Periwinkle Shores.

He looked at his cell phone and then at Rachel.

"I have to make a couple of phone calls. Why don't you take a look around the place? I won't be long. I can drive you back as soon as I'm done."

Rachel nodded and watched him go off into another room. She ran her hand over the rustic-looking railing as she climbed the stairs to the second floor.

Four bedrooms, each with their own en suite, were in each corner of the second floor. The furniture in every room was similar and looked like the wood had been carved from the trunk of a tree. Each of the four poster beds were unique in design. She wondered if Jack's talents leant themselves to furniture-making but decided not to ask. She was beginning to think that there wasn't anything Jack Harris couldn't do.

He joined her as she descended the stairs to the foyer.

"Sorry about that but I've got to get back to the house."

The sun had come out and as they walked to the truck, Rachel turned to him and held her hand up to her forehead to shield the sun from her eyes.

"Why did you take me out here, Jack? Why did you want me to see this place?"

For the first time he looked directly into her eyes, smiled and answered her question.

"Because since you didn't accept my first invitation, I thought I'd give you a second chance even though I can't offer you cake and ice cream."

She laughed at that, and in that moment she let her guard down. Jack Harris wasn't so scary after all.

CHAPTER 9

$\mathcal{T}$he forecast predicted a large snowstorm on Christmas Eve, and the fear of being separated from her sisters gave Rachel the excuse to ask Hannah and Lucy to come over early and to pack extra clothes just in case.

The shelves were bare when Rachel got to the market, but she was able to get everything on her list, nonetheless. She'd made it home just as the snowflakes started falling and was surprised to see her sisters standing at the front door.

"Hannah, where is your car?"

"Lucy thought it was a good idea to only take hers. No sense having two cars getting stuck in the snow. Is Everly next door?"

"Yes, would you run over and get her for me? Lucy and I can start putting these groceries away."

"No problem."

Hannah went to get Everly just as Jack Harris's truck pulled up in the driveway.

Rachel saw him through the window.

"What on earth…?"

Lucy followed Rachel to the front door.

"Jack. What are you doing here? You'd better get home. The snow is coming down fast."

His truck still running, he pulled his colorful knitted cap down trying to cover his ears.

"I just wanted to check on you and Everly. I thought you might not want to drive in this and I can easily with the truck. Do you need anything? Do you have enough wood for the fire? I can chop some for you if you'd like."

Lucy looked like the cat that ate the canary and Rachel found herself annoyed once again at Jack's knight-in-shining-armor gallant gesture.

"I'm fine. We're fine. Hannah and Lucy are staying with me so I'm not alone."

He held onto his hat and nodded.

Lucy couldn't contain herself any longer.

"Hey, Jack. Us women know how to chop wood. Just thought you should know."

Jack looked confused. Rachel felt embarrassed, and Hannah, now holding Everly in her arms, came through the front door in her usual upbeat and cheerful way.

"Hey, Jack. Nice hat."

"Hi, Hannah. OK. Well, if you don't need anything, I guess I'll head home. You've got my cell phone number if you need anything. I've got a plow I can add to this truck so I'm good."

Rachel wanted to sink into the floor. The interrogation she was about to endure from her sisters made her even more angry at Jack. All she could do was wave to him and quickly shut the door.

She turned to Lucy and pointed a finger at her.

"Don't. Just don't."

"What? I didn't say a thing. I think it's sweet that he keeps coming around. I think it's a bit condescending and chauvinistic but in a sweet way."

Rachel could tell that Lucy was making fun of her. Hannah

seemed oblivious to the entire event and played with Everly, who was giggling.

Putting her jacket on, Rachel walked to the back door.

"I'm going out to get more wood but there's enough by the fireplace with some newspapers to get a fire started. Lucy, why don't you get that going and then I think it's a good idea for me to defrost the soup I made the other day. This is definitely soup weather."

Hannah put Everly in her playpen and grabbed the tv remote.

"I'm ready for A Christmas Story. I think it's playing all day long on one of these stations."

After pulling her boots on, Rachel made her way out the back and to the wood pile near the carport. There was more than enough wood for this storm and several more. For a moment, she had an image of her aunt chopping wood. There was no way to know for certain, but knowing her aunt, Rachel would bet money that Kathleen chopped the wood herself.

As she continued to walk back and forth into the living room, her thoughts turned to Martin Harris and his health. She hoped he wouldn't need an ambulance during the storm. The roads were impassable and the emergency rooms would most likely get backed up if people could actually get there. She had no doubt that Jack would probably forgo the ambulance if possible and would drive his father to the hospital himself.

Once the fire was going and the soup was on the stove, Rachel got into the shower to warm up. Lucy joined Hannah on the sofa, and Everly was busy focusing on her toys. Hannah laid back on the sofa and Lucy covered her with a blanket. It didn't take long before Hannah was asleep, leaving Lucy to watch the Christmas movie by herself.

Rachel checked on the soup and then joined Lucy in the living room.

"I see Hannah didn't last very long." She whispered.

"She never does. Remember when she was a baby how easy it

was for her to go to sleep. The minute her head hit the pillow she was out."

Rachel smiled at the memory.

"Not like you. You fought going to bed right to the bitter end. Even then, once you were in your bed you'd sneak out and come downstairs to eavesdrop on whatever the adults were saying. Now that I think about it, you pretty much fought everything and everyone. You must have been a tired little kid. Always at the ready to fight whatever perceived injustice had presented itself. However did you manage to take on so many causes?"

"I had no choice. There are too many people who stay silent. That's not me. I need my voice to be heard."

Rachel decided it was time to come clean with Lucy.

"I have a confession to make."

Lucy sat up tall in her chair.

"Oh, this ought to be good. What terrible thing has Miss Goodie Two Shoes done now?"

"What does that mean?"

"It means you've never done anything wrong in your entire life. You always did what you were told."

"Well, not this time. I'm sorry, Lucy. I know that I promised, but I just couldn't ignore Martin's letters. Now that I know more about Jack's father, I feel…"

Lucy wouldn't let Rachel finish. It was like she'd been struck by a bullet and sat frozen right before a fall.

"Rachel, you promised."

"I know that, but…"

"There is no but. Those were Kathleen's letters and I specifically asked you not to pursue this."

Rachel had finally lost patience with Lucy.

"Lucy, I don't understand your reluctance. I think you've gone to a ridiculous extreme on this. Why? What is it?"

Lucy got up and started to pace the living room.

"How many of her letters did you read?"

"Most but not all. I started with the oldest and didn't get to the ones she didn't open and then there was an additional one that that she did open. It was only a few days before she died. Why? What's this all about?"

Rachel waited for Lucy to say something. She knew that her sister knew more than she had let on.

"Where are they?"

"In my bedroom."

"Get them. There's one I want you to read. Let's go into the kitchen so Hannah can't hear us. We can bring her up to speed later. Let her sleep for now."

Rachel did as she was instructed. When they were in the kitchen, she took the latest letter from Martin and began to read. Her heart raced as she absorbed his words. When she was done, she looked at Lucy and shook her head.

"No. This didn't happen."

"Yes, yes it did, and it was only a couple of days before she died. Look at the postmark."

"Martin put Stellar Seas Vineyard in Kathleen's name?"

Lucy nodded.

"Aunt Kathleen knew?"

"Yes. She knew. She told me about it. Apparently, after she got the letter telling her that the vineyard now belonged to her, she was furious with him. She sat down and wrote him a letter telling him that in no uncertain terms would she accept it. I was with her when she wrote the letter. She was a wreck about it. All Jack's life, his father blamed him for losing Aunt Kathleen. He's never treated his son with love. That awful man let Jack put his heart and soul into that vineyard and in the end took it away from him. Just like he took his plans with Kathleen away years earlier."

Rachel couldn't believe any of what she was hearing.

"How can that be? Does Jack know?"

Lucy shook her head.

"No."

Rachel put her hand to her forehead and tried to make sense of it all.

"Lucy, this is terrible. Jack will be devastated."

"Will he? As far as I can tell he won't be surprised by it at all. Nothing that evil father of his has done would surprise Jack."

"What happened when Aunt Kathleen sent the letter to Martin?"

"She never sent the letter."

"What? How do you know?"

"Because she told me. Instead of sending the letter, she went to see Martin in person. She told him that she would not take over the vineyard, and that she insisted that if he cared anything for her, he'd put the vineyard in Jack's name only."

"And?"

"He wouldn't budge. He said it was a monument to their love. What sick thinking is that? The deed is a public record and sure enough, her name is right there. It will have to be changed to reflect the estate instead of her name, but I don't know enough about all that to be sure. What I do know is that since Martin is still alive, I doubt he's said a word to Jack. Maybe now that Kathleen is gone he'll change his mind and put it in Jack's name, but I have no idea, and I don't know what to do about it. As of now, Aunt Kathleen is the sole owner of Stellar Seas Vineyards."

Rachel's head spun. She tried her best to remain calm and try to make sense of this news. Surely, there was something she could do to reverse Martin's decision. The more she thought about it the more confused she became.

"Lucy, there has to be something we can do to change Martin's mind. There's no way to know what his plans are now that Kathleen's gone. If it involves us, we have the right to know what he intends to do with the property and the business. I just don't know what we could say to him."

Rachel suddenly had a thought.

"Wait. Whatever happened to the letter that Aunt Kathleen wrote?"

Lucy didn't answer her, and it only took a few seconds before Rachel realized why.

"You have Aunt Kathleen's letter, don't you? Lucy, answer me."

"Yes, I have the letter. So what? It won't make any difference. Aunt Kathleen already told Martin she didn't want the vineyard and it didn't make a darn bit of difference."

Rachel grabbed Lucy by the shoulders.

"Lucy, the goal here is to get the vineyard in Jack's name. He deserves it. Owning that business has been his dream. He's worked his whole life for it. We don't know anything about running a vineyard and you know it. Lucy, give me the letter."

Lucy pulled away from Rachel and began to cry.

"Aunt Kathleen was everything in the world to me. She was my rock. She was like a mother to Hannah and me after Mom died. There isn't anything I wouldn't do for her. She deserves this vineyard. Martin owes her this. She loved him more than life itself, and he took that away from her. They were supposed to run the vineyard together. They had plans. All that changed when Martin got Paula pregnant and they had to get married. They'd had a few dates and the next thing she knew Kathleen's whole life changed. How is that fair?"

Suddenly Rachel realized the seriousness of what Lucy was saying. It wasn't just Kathleen's relationship with Martin that Lucy was defending; it was the close relationship that she'd shared with their aunt. The pain of losing Kathleen had been too much for Lucy. Her life ended the day their aunt died and Rachel's heart broke for her.

She reached for Lucy.

"Sweetie, Kathleen is gone. She's gone, baby, but you're still alive. You have to move on. She'd be so sad to see you like this. You have to live, honey. There's no other way. Punishing Martin means you'll be punishing Jack, and none of it will bring Kathleen back."

Lucy's legs couldn't hold her any longer. As she began to fall to the kitchen floor, Rachel grabbed her and they both went down. Lucy fell into Rachel's arms and cried like a baby.

Long ago, when Lucy was just seven years old and had scraped her knee falling off her bike, they had sat in this very embrace. As they sat in a pile of sadness this time, Rachel cried along with her sister. She knew that somewhere, wrapped in peace, forgiveness, and love their Aunt Kathleen wept with them.

CHAPTER 10

*R*achel, Lucy and Hannah set up their sleeping bags on the living room floor in front of the fireplace and reminisced about Christmases past and the fun they'd had growing up. Rachel marveled at how brave Lucy was. She'd suffered a loss much larger than either she or Hannah had but put her sadness away for the sake of their younger sister and Everly.

The storm outside had reached epic proportions. All through the night they watched Christmas movies, drank eggnog with brandy and when they couldn't keep their eyes open one minute longer, fell asleep in front of the Christmas tree waiting for Santa Claus. In the morning, the sun came out, and by noon, the neighborhood children were already outside building snowmen.

Rachel stopped by Christine's to make sure she had survived the storm, and to invite her to come over for Christmas dinner if she didn't already have plans. Fortunately, her children and grandchildren drove down before the storm to keep her company.

Lucy already had the turkey in the oven before they opened their gifts, making the house smell wonderful.

"Rachel, how many pictures of Everly are you going to take? That cell phone has only so much space on it," Hannah asked.

"As many as this cell phone can hold. That's how many," Rachel said.

With every wrapping paper and ribbon pulled, Rachel had to get a photo of it. Toys as well as clothes were strewn around the floor. Hannah, ever the neat one in the family, filled the plastic trash bag with paper, ribbons and bows and anything else that resulted in Everly's demolishing of the living room.

Lucy followed Rachel into the kitchen to check on the turkey.

"So, when are you going to see Martin?"

"Probably tomorrow. No time like the present."

Lucy looked down at the floor.

"I'll get that letter for you. You might as well bring it with you. I guess it could be used as leverage, although I don't know if it will work."

Rachel hugged Lucy.

"Thank you. It's worth a try. For Jack's sake, I have to do it."

Lucy smiled and cocked her head to the side.

"So, exactly what's going on between you and Jack? At first, I thought you hated the guy. Now, I'm not so sure."

Rachel shook her head.

"Nothing is going on between us. We're friends that's all. Honestly, Lucy, do you really think I'd fall back into another relationship after Brian? I still have battle wounds and trust me, they're going to take a long time to heal."

True to her word, Lucy gave Rachel Kathleen's letter. Lucy was right, everything in the letter spelled out Kathleen's intentions to reject Martin's proposal of placing Stellar Seas Vineyards in her name.

Rachel took her time trying to find the right words to say to

Martin. Not only would she have to have a private conversation with the man, but she'd also need to do it when Jack wasn't around. It seemed an impossible task, when Lucy came up with the idea of asking Jack to look at another plumbing problem at Rachel's.

"That would work except I don't have any leaks that need attention."

The women still hadn't told Hannah everything, so Rachel and Lucy asked Oliver to get involved by asking Jack to have a drink with him after work and would explain everything to him at a later time. Rachel refused to share her plan with anyone other than Lucy, at least for the time being.

"What did he say?" Rachel asked as Lucy stood in front of the refrigerator looking for something to eat.

"Oliver said it might look unusual if he asks Jack to go out for a beer because he's never done it before."

"So?"

"He said he'd text me the minute Jack answered him. That was two hours ago. Don't you have leftover turkey in here? We didn't finish it all, did we?"

"Bottom shelf, right side."

Lucy squealed with glee when she found the turkey.

"I'm so hungry I could eat a horse. I didn't have any breakfast this morning."

Snow plows continued up and down the street trying to make a wider path for cars. The snowbanks were tall and Lucy, being the shortest in the family could barely look over them.

"It's really slow going on the roads. I wish it would warm up a little. If it stays cold out there, the snow will never melt."

Lucy's cell phone buzzed with a response from Oliver.

It's a go. I'm meeting Jack at six o'clock at The Pearl.

"Well, there's your answer. You'll be meeting Martin at six. Do you want me to go with you? If the two of us go, maybe he'll feel the pressure to do the right thing."

Rachel shook her head.

"No. I can do it. Would you stay with Everly when I go? When I get back I want to tell you everything that happened and I'd rather do it in person instead of the phone."

"No problem. You don't mind if I make myself another turkey dinner tonight do you?"

Rachel laughed.

"Help yourself. You and I both know you'd be back for more even if you weren't watching Everly."

Rachel looked in the mirror and straightened her green bandana. Her emerald drop earrings completed her look and for the first time she noticed how much her wild hair reminded her of her aunt's. She hated to admit it, but she was nervous. So much of Jack's future depended on her getting through to Martin.

Even if he wouldn't cooperate, Rachel had a plan to make things right for Jack, but it would be easier for her if Martin agreed to put the vineyard in Jack's name instead of her aunt's.

She put Kathleen's letter in her purse and bundled up against the cold. Lucy and Everly were watching cartoons in the living room.

"Well, I guess I'm off. Wish me luck."

Lucy smiled at Rachel.

"I hate to say this, but you need more than luck. I'd say a miracle is in order."

Rachel agreed, but one way or another, she drew comfort in knowing that her aunt would be proud of her actions. The glare of the sun against the snow made it difficult to see so Rachel put her sunglasses on and started the car.

Stellar Seas Vineyards was only ten minutes from her house and there was no gate entrance leading to the main house so she drove up to the front and parked her car. She got out of the car and walked up to the front door and, after taking a deep breath, rang the doorbell.

She was shocked to see Martin answer the door. She'd assumed a housekeeper would show her in.

"I wondered how long it would take for you to come here. Come in."

He opened the door wider and Rachel stepped inside.

"Let's go into the living room. My housekeeper just made a nice fire for me. We can sit there."

Rachel chose a chair in front of the fireplace and Martin selected the one across from her.

"Would you like some tea?"

Rachel shook her head.

"No. Thank you."

Martin looked at Rachel and smiled.

"My, how much you look like her.

"You were expecting me?"

"I'd hoped not to, but I didn't know if Kathleen told any of you girls of my intention. How did you find out about the deed? I asked my attorney to keep this quiet until my death for obvious reasons."

Rachel's eyebrow raised in surprised.

"Obvious reasons? You mean like your only son finding out?"

"You don't approve?"

"I don't, and neither did my aunt and I know she told you so."

Martin looked surprised at her statement.

"Then, she did tell you girls about our discussion?"

"She told my sister Lucy and of course there's the letter."

He flinched as if she'd just stabbed him with something sharp.

"What letter?

"My aunt wrote her feelings about your plan in a letter. I assume she thought it would be proof of her rejection of your proposal to deed the property to her. She wanted control of her life since you'd already taken so much from her. The letter proves she didn't approve of your plan."

"That's ridiculous. I'm not doing any harm to you girls by giving you the vineyard. How ungrateful. You'd think you'd be happy to have such an inheritance. You'll be wealthy with this transaction."

"Mr. Harris, you never got to read this letter, so there's something in it that you don't know. Apparently my aunt and your wife became good friends over the years. Your wife knew how much you'd disapprove, so they kept their friendship from you. Your wife often lamented the fact that you'd blamed Jack for losing Kathleen. You didn't know that did you?"

Martin's frail body got up from his chair and walked closer to the fire.

"No. I didn't know they were friends. How does any of that have anything to do with this?"

"You've been terrible to Jack, you betrayed your wife with this fantasy, and now you're doing something even Kathleen disapproved of, not to mention that in the end my sisters and I won't own the vineyard after all. If you won't cooperate, we plan to sell it to Jack for one dollar after you've died."

Rachel didn't think it possible, but Martin stood tall in defiance and anger. He knew he was beat but he stubbornly refused to look as if she'd won.

She stood as well and faced him.

"Was it worth it? Was living this fantasy worth losing everything? Why not put the vineyard in Jack's name now and find a way to connect with your son in the months you have left? The vineyard isn't the only thing you can give Jack, Mr. Harris. How about a bit of your love and an apology for not being a good father all these years?"

He sat back in his chair and looked at her.

"I can see you and your sisters running this place, but you're right. None of this has been Jack's fault. That's not the point."

Rachel had always planned to hit Martin with an accusation that no one thus far had said aloud."

"It wasn't love that drove you to do this. It was pride and ego, and in the end it probably killed Kathleen."

The shocked look on Martin's face told Rachel that she'd hit the very nerve she'd come to attack.

"No. Don't say that. I loved her. I never meant…"

"What you did caused her a great deal of stress. That had to have taken a toll on her health…on her heart. If you don't do what my aunt and your wife wanted, you'll go to your grave with that knowledge."

As small a man as Martin Harris was, he now looked tiny and defeated.

"I'll change the deed and have my lawyers get in touch." He whispered.

"Jack loves this vineyard Mr. Harris. He's earned the right to own it."

Martin nodded and didn't say anything more until she walked towards the door.

"You're more like your aunt than I realized."

She'd always believed that her sister Lucy was most like Kathleen, but suddenly she felt her aunt's hand on her shoulder, guiding her way.

Rachel nodded.

"Yes. I am."

CHAPTER 11

As they entered the new year, the sisters waited for word from Martin's attorney, but nothing came.

Rachel and Lucy explained everything to Hannah.

"You guys don't have to treat me like I'm a child. You should have told me when you found out."

"You're right," Rachel said.

Lucy tried to explain.

"We're sorry, honey, we should have told you, but there was so much going on, we didn't know what was going to happen. From now on, all three of us will share everything."

"So, it's been over a week, has his lawyer contacted you?"

Rachel shook her head.

"Nope. We haven't heard a thing. I really hope he keeps his promise to change the deed."

Just then, Oliver was standing at the front door.

"Have you guys heard the news?"

"What?"

"Jack's father Martin Harris died day before yesterday."

Rachel looked at Lucy and Hannah and then back at Oliver.

"Are you sure? How did you find out?"

"Craig, my electrician called me this morning. I know you guys have something going on with Jack. I came right over here as soon as I heard. I've got to run though. I'm working on the old Congregational church on Main. Lots of restoration there."

Oliver kissed Hannah before leaving. As soon as he closed the door behind him, the conversation turned to the shocking news.

"What are we going to do?" asked Lucy.

Rachel shook her head.

"I have no idea. I don't know whether Martin changed the deed or not and there's no way to find out. I don't even know who his attorney is and besides, the man wouldn't talk to me about his private dealings with his client. That information is privileged."

Lucy said what all of them were thinking.

"Looks like there's nothing to do but wait."

Rachel sighed and then looked at her.

"Yeah, but wait for what? Either the attorney will get in touch or Jack's going to show up madder than..."

Hannah stopped her.

"Don't say it, Rachel. We get the point."

When the obituary showed up online, Rachel, Lucy and Hannah prepared themselves for the inevitable awkwardness at the funeral. They had no idea what Martin did or didn't do and they were in the dark knowing if Jack had any information on the vineyard's fate. All they knew was that a possible confrontation with Jack was only days away.

Several hundred people attended the funeral. There was no social gathering after the cemetery, in keeping with Martin's request. Several people got up in front of the church to speak about him, but Jack wasn't one of them. He wore sunglasses and never smiled once during the entire event. He never approached

Rachel or her sisters and as far as she could tell, there was little emotion from him.

Lucy leaned close to Rachel and whispered.

"I don't know about you, but if I was a betting person, I'd say Jack Harris isn't very happy with us right now."

Rachel felt awful. Odds were that Stellar Seas Vineyard now belonged to her, Lucy and Hannah, and although they had little interest in running the place, Rachel had no idea how she would approach the sale of the business to its rightful owner.

She tried to imagine how Jack must feel. Pride alone would prevent him from accepting her gift. She didn't know how she knew, she just knew, and it pained her to think there wasn't much that she could do to remedy the situation.

Oliver stood next to Hannah and when the funeral was over, he drove her back home, while Rachel drove Lucy home and then picked up Everly from Christine's place.

"How was she?"

"Rachel, I swear little Everly is the happiest baby I've ever known. She wasn't a bit of trouble at all."

"Thank you for watching her. You're a godsend."

"How was the funeral?"

"Oh, you know how they are. Awful."

"Well, at least Martin wasn't there."

"What do you mean?"

"Oh, honey, it's much too cold. The ground is frozen. They just go through the ceremony and the motions just to acknowledge the family's loss. The community needs closure. Martin is probably back at the funeral home where he'll stay until the ground thaws."

As morbid as Christine's words were, it was the first time in days that Rachel felt like laughing. She knew it was inappropriate but when she looked at Christine who was trying to hold back a snicker, she burst into laughing out loud.

For several minutes, the two women laughed so hard that

Everly assumed something wonderful happened and joined them. Her giggles only made Rachel and Christine laugh harder, and after their sides hurt and their faces were wet with tears, they stopped and Christine made the sign of the cross and looked up to ask for forgiveness.

Days went by with no word from either Jack or Martin's attorney. Rachel was beside herself. She couldn't control any of what was happening, so in the end, she decided to shift her focus onto other things—things she could control.

The house badly needed furniture. She'd kept a few pieces including the sofa and rocking chair in the living room, but that was only so that she'd have some place to sit.

She decided that a list of items that she needed to buy would be a good idea, so she got a piece of paper and a pen and began walking around the house thinking of what was necessary to live. She didn't want to spend a lot of her money so only the bare necessities would be purchased.

After making her list, she looked at the clock. Thirty minutes had passed and her stress about Jack was building. It was too cold for a walk, so she called Lucy to see if she wanted to go to the Old Navy store in Barnstable.

"Sure. I'm not doing anything but alternating between looking at the clock and my cell phone waiting for news. I'll be right over."

When Lucy arrived, Rachel and Everly already had their coats on and were ready to go. Lucy put Everly's stroller into the trunk and got back into the car. Fastening Everly into her car seat Rachel looked out the back window and saw Jack's truck pull up behind Lucy's car.

"Oh my God, Rachel. It's Jack."

Rachel sighed. "Why do I think we're not going to the mall?"

She stood frozen in place beside the car and waited for Jack to approach her.

"We need to talk."

"Now? Lucy is here. We were going to take Everly shopping in Barnstable."

Rachel could see this was the moment she both needed and dreaded. She looked at Everly and then back at Lucy.

"Any chance you might...?"

"Say no more. I'll call you later."

Rachel waved as Lucy pulled out of the driveway. She unlocked the front door and Jack followed her inside.

"I think you know why I'm here."

Rachel nodded.

"I do."

"How long were you going to wait before talking to me about your visit with my father?"

"He told you about that?"

"He did. He also told me what you both talked about. What made you think you could do that?"

Rachel was confused. She was bordering on anger instead of fear.

"Do what exactly?"

"Tell him that he needed to be a better father to me."

"Jack. Listen to me. I didn't go to see your father to talk to him about his parenting skills. That's between the two of you. My family never wanted to be involved with your family issues. Your father dragged us into it by deeding the vineyard to my aunt. I was there to tell him that we don't want it even though my aunt already told him the same thing before she died."

"What are you talking about?"

"Didn't your father explain why I was there?"

"Dad told me that you came to see him because my mother and your aunt were good friends. He said that my mother confided in Kathleen a lot. Apparently, it hurt her that Dad and I weren't very close and that somehow you took it upon yourself to tell my father about it. What's this about the vineyard being deeded to your aunt's estate?"

She sat on a sofa and put her head in her hands. She tried to make sense of this news.

Why would Martin say such a thing to Jack and then leave out the most important reason for her coming to see him?

Jack sat next to her and waited. When she looked up at him, he was smiling.

"Why are you smiling? This whole thing is a mess. I think the best thing I can do is start at the beginning. I'll try to explain as best I can, based on what I know. It all started when I found your father's letters to my aunt. Maybe I should go get them so you can read them yourself."

She got up and started for the bedroom when he grabbed her arm and pulled her back down.

"You don't need to get the letters. I know about them, and I know what my father wrote to your aunt. I'm only sorry that you've had to struggle with this. You came back home to start your life over with your daughter and got mixed up in this soap opera drama that is the romantic triangle of Paula, Martin and Kathleen."

"How long have you known about this?"

"Since my mother told me. She knew because your aunt told her. It's true that my mother and Kathleen were very good friends. That friendship created a bond that trickled down to me. Your aunt and uncle became an extended family for me. Matthew was like a father to me and Kathleen, well, she was a special lady. She practically raised me. Don't you remember the two of us playing in the driveway when we were kids?"

Stunned, she didn't know what to say. All she could do was shake her head.

"I was a lot taller than you and we had that little car we'd have to pump with our feet. You couldn't reach the pedals so I had to push you. I used to love it when you'd visit your aunt. It meant I got to see you again. My parents knew I was over here all the time. That's why I invited you to my birthday party. I was teasing you the other day when I said you didn't respond. You couldn't come because you were sick with a cold."

Rachel wanted to hit him. It felt like Jack had been keeping so much from her, but now there was only one issue left to address.

"What about the vineyard, Jack?"

"Stellar Seas Vineyards is now owned jointly by Rachel Adams and Jack Harris. It's what my father wanted. It's what your aunt would want, and most importantly, it's what I want."

"Jack, I don't know a thing about running a vineyard. This is a mistake. What could you be thinking?"

He stood and reached for her. She placed her hand in his and wondered where he was taking her.

"I can teach you. Starting now. Come with me."

CHAPTER 12

*R*achel felt embarrassed that she not only knew nothing about Stellar Seas Vineyard, but also knew nothing about wine. She knew what she liked, and as far as Jack was concerned, that was an excellent start.

As they walked in the darkened room passing oak barrels of wine, Jack explained.

"There's a lot to learn I grant you, but my question to you, Rachel, is do you want to learn? Can you see yourself as part owner of this vineyard?"

"Oh, Jack this was never my plan. I didn't go to see your father to get my name on the deed. I hope you believe me."

"Of course I do. Dad told me that you planned to sell your aunt's share to me for $1.00. I've known for several days now that you and your sisters weren't trying to take advantage of the situation. I have to admit, at first I didn't like the idea of having a partner. Dad and I talked about it. He knew that you knew nothing about growing grapes or wine. He asked me what I wanted. He said he'd do whatever I wanted and nothing else."

Rachel braced herself for a possibility that she hadn't allowed herself to admit until now—that Martin's plan would succeed after all.

"Ultimately, my father let me make the decision about the future of this land. I've spent the last three days asking myself what I want the legacy of this place to be. In the end, I believe it is a great idea for both our families that we share in its future. I want you to be my business partner. The history of this vineyard is inextricably joined with our two families. But I won't force your hand. If you say no, then that's the end of it. What do you want? Isn't it time you ask yourself the same question I did?"

Rachel hadn't given much thought to her career. She'd been a schoolteacher most of her adult life. She had been a good student and teacher, and a quick learner. After her divorce her only concern was Everly and making a good home for her.

Kathleen had gifted her more than she ever expected and now, Rachel was faced with accepting more than just the house. She had to decide what she wanted the next several years to look like, and what she might leave to her daughter one day.

"Would I be crazy and presumptuous to talk about us working together as friends only? I mean, am I nuts or is there something going on between us?"

Jack smiled at her.

"You're not nuts. Is that a deal-breaker?"

"I'm not ready, Jack."

"That's fine. I'll go slow."

She laughed at that.

"I'm serious. If I do this, then it's got to be platonic between us. I have Everly to think about and a new roof to pay for. I don't want our working together to assume there's anything more."

Jack nodded.

"I understand. Do we have a deal?"

He extended his hand and waited for Rachel to accept it.

She took his hand in a business handshake.

"I must be crazy, but yes, we have a deal."

"Great. Now, let me give you a taste of my favorite wine."

He got two glasses and showed her the bottle. A mermaid holding a glass of wine on the label showed various pastel colors surrounding her.

"What a pretty bottle. I love the name—Mermaid's Tears."

"This is the first wine our vineyard ever produced. Of course it's not the 1970 vintage. That wouldn't taste very good. This is our signature wine and the 2018 vintage."

He filled their glasses and showed Rachel how to smell the wine and take in only a small amount of the precious liquid before swallowing.

"My father named this wine after Kathleen's favorite hobby— collecting sea glass."

Rachel knew the significance of the name and felt it appropriate that she would join the vineyard family. She smiled and did exactly as Jack asked and thought about the next few years of her life and what it would look like. Having a better grasp of the difference between a dream and a plan, she chose.

It was simple. In time, she knew she wouldn't be the only Adams woman running Stellar Seas Vineyards. After all, the rest of the descendants of the original Sea Glass Girl belonged on this land just as much as she did.

Rachel, Lucy, Hannah and Everly Brooke Adams—the Sea Glass Girls, and the memory of a woman who understood the importance of family, and the call of the sea.

THE END

Thank you for reading
Christmas on the Cape - A Novella.

Book 2 in the Periwinkle Shores series
The Sea Glass Girls will release in March 2023.

ABOUT THE AUTHOR

Annie Cabot is the author of contemporary women's fiction and family sagas. Annie writes about friendships and family relationships, that bring inspiration and hope to others.

Annie Cabot is the pen name for the writer Patricia Pauletti (Patti) who, for the last seven years, has been the co-author of several paranormal mystery books under the pen name Juliette Harper. A lover of all things happily ever after, it was only a matter of time before she began to write what was in her heart, and so, the pen name Annie Cabot was born.

When she's not writing, Annie and her husband like to travel. Winters always involve time away on Captiva Island, Florida where she continues to get inspiration for her novels.

Annie lives in Massachusetts with her husband and furbaby Otis.

For more information visit anniecabot.com

ALSO BY ANNIE CABOT

THE CAPTIVA ISLAND SERIES

*Where you will meet The Wheeler Family and a cast of unforgettable characters
you will fall in love with.*

Book One: KEY LIME GARDEN INN

Book Two: A CAPTIVA WEDDING

Book Three: CAPTIVA MEMORIES

Book Four: CAPTIVA CHRISTMAS

Book Five in this series:

CAPTIVA NIGHTS

Will release February 2023.

Made in United States
North Haven, CT
29 September 2023

42141019R00054